The Lost Treasure of Tuckernuck

The LOST TRE

of

TUCKE

Illustrated by

EMILY FAIRLIE

ASURE RNUCK

ANTONIO JAVIER CAPARO

KT KATHERINE TEGEN BOOKS
An Imprint of HarperCollins Publishers

Katherine Tegen Books is an imprint of HarperCollins Publishers.

The Lost Treasure of Tuckernuck
Text copyright © 2012 by Emily Ecton
Illustrations copyright © 2012 by Antonio Javier Caparo

Library of Congress Cataloging-in-Publication Data is available.
ISBN 978-0-06-211890-5

Typography by Erin Fitzsimmons
12 13 14 15 16 LP/RRDH   10 9 8 7 6 5 4 3 2 1

First Edition

To my fellow Fairlies:

Hank and Barbara,
Sarah and Robert,
and Zuzu, Pepper, and Binky

The Lost Treasure of Tuckernuck

Maria Tutweiler stood on the stage and gazed out at the students seated before her. As Mrs. Reynolds read her opening statement, Principal Tutweiler's eyes moved from student to student. Who would be the one? Principal Tutweiler suppressed a smile. The school had been a wonderful idea. Her plans had come together better than she'd ever dreamed.

Mrs. Reynolds finished her remarks, and Principal Tutweiler took the podium. She cleared her throat. "Welcome, Tuckernuckers! You are the first, the proud students who will lead future generations and carry this school to greatness. But first, a challenge. Who among you can unravel the puzzle? To reveal what is hidden, you will need a great many things—courage, persistence, intelligence, and creativity. But to begin your journey, all you need is Hope. The prize? A treasure beyond bounds!"

Principal Tutweiler paused in satisfaction as ripples of excitement washed over the student body. The Tuckernuck challenge had been issued. Now all she had to do was sit back and watch.

PART ONE
THE CHALLENGE

EIGHTY YEARS LATER . . .

EIGHTY YEARS LATER . . .

New Student Orientation Letter, page two

> And finally, students, remember to stop
> in the lobby and read school founder
> Maria Tutweiler's challenge for yourself.
> Remember, just because the puzzle hasn't
> been solved yet doesn't mean it won't be
> solved. Maybe by YOU!
> Your Princi"PAL"
> Martin Winkle
> Tuckernuck's Number One Clucker!

Tuckernuck Hall was seriously messed up. Maybe there was something in the water. Laurie didn't know how else to explain everybody getting so caught up in a lame nonexistent challenge.

Her parents had gone to Tuckernuck, so that meant that Laurie had to go too. Never mind that her best friend in the world, Kimmy Baranski, was going to Hamilton Junior High, where they didn't have dumb things like school challenges. Nope, Laurie had to be a stupid Clucker and get all excited about some dumb lost treasure she'd heard about a thousand times, but which probably didn't even exist.

Laurie didn't know why she was even bothering to read the challenge. She was going to need all her brain power to convince her mom to let her transfer to Hamilton. Preferably before the next bell.

She'd ditched lunch when Tessa Tysinger started figuring out the calorie count in her ice cubes and telling Laurie to dye what Tessa called her dishwater blond hair. And instead of trying to find a new place to sit, she'd wandered around until she ended up staring at the plaque engraved with Maria Tutweiler's famous challenge.

She chewed on her lower lip and read the last line of the challenge again.

". . . to begin your journey, all you need is Hope," Laurie muttered to herself. There was something about that last line, but she couldn't quite get it. It had been bothering her since that morning, when she'd read the challenge on her way to homeroom. Not that she was taking the whole treasure thing seriously, of course.

"So you're trying to find the treasure too?" A voice behind her interrupted her train of thought. Crud. Busted.

Calliope Judkin was standing two steps behind her, looking up at the plaque. "Got any ideas?"

Laurie shrugged. Like she was going to tell Calliope Judkin if she did. "Some."

Calliope nodded. "Me too. I did some investigative work over the summer, and I've got a few theories. Along with a highly placed source in the school system, if you know what I mean. Insider tips." She patted a notebook she was carrying and then carefully tucked it back in with her books.

Last year Calliope had decided she was going to be a reporter, and she had proceeded to make everyone's life miserable with her investigations ever since. "I just may be the one to crack this thing."

"Huh," Laurie said. She didn't know what to say. If she had to put money on anyone finding the treasure, Calliope Judkin would be the smart bet. She was also the last person Laurie would ever bet on.

Calliope glanced at her watch. "Oh, gotta run. See you!" She trotted off down the hall.

Laurie frowned. Highly placed source? Forget the treasure, if she could beat Calliope, that would make it all worthwhile. Not that Calliope wasn't nice—she was. But how many things did that girl need to win?

She was already the fifth-grade spelling bee and geography bee champion, winner of the local VFW's "What America Means to Me" elementary school essay contest, grand prize winner in the science fair three years running, and cast in the lead role of the Statue of Liberty in the fifth-grade play, *Our Glorious Nation*. It was that last one that really rankled. Laurie was cast in the minor role of Rhode Island. And everybody knows Rhode Island doesn't get any good lines.

Just once, Laurie wanted to be the winner, the top dog. Top dogs didn't worry about where to eat lunch or get unsolicited makeover advice or get cast as the tiniest state. Plus, finding the treasure would be a good way to pass the time until she managed to get that transfer.

Laurie dug in her backpack and pulled out the handout Principal Winkle had given them at the assembly that morning.

Welcome to the flock, new Tuckernuckers! Your fellow students and I are very excited to welcome you to the school. You may have heard that, sadly, the school is in danger of shutting down, but until it does, you are

Tuckernuck Cluckers, brave and true. So please memorize the attached pages—you'll need to know the words to the Tuckernuck Clucker Anthem and pledge by heart! Our next assembly is coming up, so get clucking!

Laurie crumpled up Principal Winkle's memo and tossed it into the trash can in the lobby. There was no way she was studying some dumb Clucker anthem.

Laurie glared at the portrait of Maria Tutweiler hanging above the plaque. "Your stupid challenge doesn't say anything! How is this even a challenge? A challenge to what?"

Laurie took a deep breath and focused on the plaque. All you need is Hope.

And it was like a lightbulb going off.

With a quick glance around to make sure that there were no nosy administrators lurking in the shadows, Laurie took out her cell phone and dialed quickly. Sure, it was just for emergencies, but if solving the Tuckernuck challenge wasn't an emergency, she didn't know what was. Laurie smirked. And Calliope thought she was so hot.

"What's up?" Laurie's brother Jack's voice came through the phone. He sounded muffled, like he was trying to be quiet. Laurie hoped he was at lunch too, and not in some class. Not that it really mattered, with news like hers.

Laurie tried not to sound smug. "Yeah, the challenge? Totally solved it." Well, not too smug anyway.

"Really? Awesome. So where's the treasure?" Somehow Jack didn't sound as excited as she thought he'd be. Maybe they had a bad connection.

"Well, I'm not sure yet, but I solved the challenge. It's so obvious. That last line? All you need is Hope? Well, hope is capitalized, like a name. Get it?"

Jack didn't say anything. Laurie figured he must be speechless and reeling in shock.

"The challenge is talking about a person named Hope, see? All I have to do is figure out who Hope was, and voilà! Challenge solved." Laurie scanned the paintings in the lobby. "She's probably a chick in one of these paintings."

Jack still wasn't saying anything. Laurie was getting irritated. Talk about a bad sport.

"Hello?" Laurie said impatiently.

Jack cleared his throat. "You've never really looked at

the paintings in the school, have you?"

What was to look at? She'd been in the school a thousand times. They were regular paintings.

"Well, not exactly . . ." Laurie trailed off as the painting opposite Maria Tutweiler's portrait caught her eye. It was the biggest painting in the room, with the best location. And it was of a chicken.

"What the . . . is that a—"

"Chicken?" Jack cut in. "Yeah, there's a big ol' painting of a chicken named Hilda. Tutweiler painted it herself. That the one you're looking at?"

"Uh." Laurie stared at the painting. It wasn't even a cute chicken. It looked like it had the chicken mange. And insomnia, for a couple of weeks at least, if the bags under its eyes were any indication. And a serious case of stomach cramps. And what kind of name was Hilda for a chicken?

Laurie did a quick art survey. She didn't know how she'd been coming here all those years without noticing. This school was even weirder than she'd realized. Laurie'd heard people complain about the jumble of different styles before, but she'd never taken time to notice what a mess the decor was. And the other paintings were just as useless, unless there was a famous fruit basket or dancing frog or oak tree named Hope that Laurie wasn't familiar with.

"Funny thing there. Not a Hope in any of the paintings. In fact, not a Hope in the whole history of the school, as far as I can tell. No teachers, no Tutweiler siblings, nothing." Jack laughed. "Nice try, Laur, but that's way too obvious. If the challenge was that easy, don't you think it would've been solved by now?"

"Gotta go," Laurie muttered, flipping her phone shut. Just in time too—Miss Abernathy was coming around the corner, and word on the street was that she had a whole desk drawer filled with confiscated cell phones. Or at least that's what Hannah Stoller said, and with the amount of text messaging Hannah did, she should know. Laurie glared at her and then glared spitefully at Hilda the mutant chicken before heading back to Mrs. Hutchins's room.

They were getting their classroom assignments after lunch—apparently Mrs. Hutchins thought they were all still in kindergarten—but if she was lucky, she'd get something cool. Birthday Planner or Social Networking Coordinator. Something to make life bearable until her transfer came through.

It's not like it could get any worse.

Classroom Assignment Sheet
Mrs. Hutchins's sixth-grade class

Remember, these assignments are very important, so take them seriously!

Office Liaison: Calliope Judkin

Attendance Monitor: Troy Hopkins

Class Media Expert: Sheila Weston

Social Networking Coordinators: Tessa Tysinger, Hannah Stoller

Gerbil Monitors: Bud Wallace, Laurie Madison

Supply Monitor: Mariah Jeffries

Birthday Planner: Trinity Harbaugh

Homework Coordinator: Sam Silver

Laurie had tried to be a good sport. She'd flapped her arms in the morning assembly. She'd clucked. She'd tried to put on a happy face. But this was just too much. This was beyond the call of duty.

No one should have to endure gerbil duty.

"So once you get to know Ponch and Jon, you'll see that they're feisty, but they shouldn't give you much trouble." Mrs. Hutchins smiled at Laurie and held out

Ponch (or Jon) encouragingly. "They just have some quirks you should be aware of. I know you'll do fine."

Laurie gave a weak smile, doing her best to ignore the evil malicious glare Jon (or Ponch) was shooting in her direction. Regular gerbils were one thing, but Ponch and Jon had gotten a reputation. Word around school was the kid who drew gerbil duty last year had lost a finger.

Laurie went back to work on a mental list of reasons her mom should let her transfer. Yeah, she should probably listen to what Mrs. Hutchins was saying. As Gerbil Monitor Number Two, she probably needed to know all of the vital gerbil-related information that Mrs. Hutchins was giving her. But with any luck, somebody else would be stuck with the title Gerbil Monitor Number Two, and she'd be enjoying life as a ten-fingered Hamilton Junior High student.

". . . so do you think you're ready to take over the official gerbil duties tomorrow?" Mrs. Hutchins said, grinning and patting Ponch (or Jon) on the head while Jon (or Ponch) glared at Laurie from the glass wall of his aquarium. It was hard to tell them apart. They were both cleverly disguised as your basic brown standard-issue classroom gerbils. With attitude. Whoever Mrs. Hutchins was holding bared his dripping fangs at her. Laurie shuddered. Yeah, no way was she touching that thing.

Bud Wallace cleared his throat and gave a serious nod, looking every bit the sixth grade butt-kisser he was. "I'm willing and able," Bud said, his voice cracking on the last word. It kind of spoiled the whole brown-nosing effect.

Laurie bit her lip so she wouldn't laugh. "Sure thing. No prob," she agreed. What difference did it make what she said? This time tomorrow she'd be a Hamilton Hornet. Once her mom heard her reasons for transferring, Tuckernuck wouldn't stand a chance.

Reasons I Should Be Able to Transfer Schools by Laurie Madison, grade six

1. I go to Tuckernuck Hall Intermediate. Our mascot is a chicken. We're called the Tuckernuck Cluckers. Need I say more?
2. Kimmy Baranski, my best friend since birth (okay, not really, but practically), is going to Hamilton Junior High. Not Tuckernuck.
3. The school is probably going to be shut down anyway, so why not reduce the trauma of changing schools and do it early

in the year?

4. Tuckernuck was founded by a confirmed crazy woman, who supposedly hid a treasure in the school, which nobody has found in a gazillion years and probably doesn't even exist. Crazy woman school = bad influence.

5. Two words: gerbil duty.

"Absolutely not, Laurie. You're staying at Tuckernuck, and that's final." Mrs. Madison stabbed a piece of meat loaf decisively.

"But *Mom*!" Laurie shrieked. "I can't!" She couldn't believe this was happening. Didn't her mom understand? Hadn't she seen the list? That number three, with the possible trauma? That was genius! Who could argue with possible trauma?

"Inside voice, Laurie," Mr. Madison said into his mashed potatoes.

Laurie nodded and gaped at her parents. She had never thought they could be so cold and heartless.

"You're not going to be traumatized, Laurie." Mrs. Madison frowned and chewed her meat loaf. "You'll be just fine."

It was like she was made of ice, she was so cold. Like the Ice Queen. Or maybe the White Witch. Whichever it was, it wasn't good.

"Give it up, Laurie." Jack munched on a piece of bread and stared at her. "The Clucker whining is getting pretty old."

Laurie glared at him. He was so not helping. "But...," Laurie stammered. This would be the perfect time to come up with a convincing new argument, but she had nothing. That list was her last shot.

Mrs. Madison sighed and wiped her mouth on her napkin. "Laurie, I'll say it one more time. I was a Clucker. Your dad was a Clucker. Your granddad was a Clucker. It's in your blood."

Over my dead body, Laurie thought, scowling at the saltshaker.

"What happened? You were always excited to go to Tuckernuck. Remember? You wanted to find the treasure...."

"When I was five, maybe," Laurie muttered under her breath. "When I was dumb enough to think it was real."

"What was that?" Mrs. Madison's voice was sharp. Laurie knew she was pushing it. If there was one thing

Laurie's mom had, it was school spirit.

"Good school, Tuckernuck," Mr. Madison said through a mouthful of lima beans. "No shame in being a Tuckernuck Clucker, Laurie."

Laurie put on her sad clown face. Mom could never resist a sad clown. One look at the rec room decor would tell you that much. "The school is probably closing anyway! It's been all over the news. It's not like I'd ever get to be a full-fledged Clucker like you guys, so why not just let me go to Hamilton now? Think of the months of readjustment time you'd save me." Laurie played her trump card. "My grades could suffer, you know."

Mrs. Madison rolled her eyes. Apparently the powers of the sad clown face were limited. "Nice try, Laurie, but no, I'm sorry. We think positively in this house, and what kind of Cluckers would we be if we just gave up on Tuckernuck? You're not changing schools. It's final." She got up and went into the kitchen.

Laurie scowled harder and stared into her plate. The gravy was pooling on one side, and it almost looked like a silhouette of a gerbil. Staring at her. Mocking her.

"You guys are lame," she muttered gloomily. "I have gerbil duty, you know. Hamilton doesn't force kids to do gerbil duty."

A flash of understanding suddenly shot across Jack's face. Ponch and Jon had quite the reputation. "Gerbil duty by yourself? Man, sorry, Laurie." Jack was one of the few people who understood Laurie's pet philosophy—mainly, that gerbils didn't qualify.

"Not by myself. With a partner." Laurie lifted her eyes and glared at Jack. "Bud Wallace."

Jack unsuccessfully attempted to stifle a laugh. "Bud Wallace? Oh, man." He wiped his nose. Something had obviously taken the wrong path during the stifling.

"Who's this?" Mrs. Madison asked as she came back in.

"Short kid, light brown hair, middle school public enemy number one," Jack snickered.

Mr. Madison perked up, partly because Mrs. Madison had returned with bowls of ice cream, but mostly because of the name. "Is that Horace Wallace's son?"

"Oh, yeah," Laurie said.

"How's he doing?" Mr. Madison reached for the chocolate sauce. "Haven't seen much of him since his wife died."

"How am I supposed to know?" Laurie said. "I go to school with Bud, not his dad."

"Even I know about Bud Wallace," Jack said,

grinning. "He's the one who got them to ban sweets in school, right?"

Laurie nodded. Everyone knew about Bud Wallace. The year before, Bud had done a science fair project on healthy eating and the bad effects of sugar. He got so into it that he and his dad had petitioned the school board to ban candy, soda, and other junk foods from schools in the entire district. Unfortunately for Bud, it worked. Half the class still wasn't talking to him.

"Well, if he's your partner, problem solved. He won't let you touch those little guys in case you do something to ruin his grades. You're golden."

Laurie felt a glimmer of hope. "You think so?"

Jack nodded, taking a bowl of ice cream. "Definitely. Plus you can use him as a human shield when Ponch and Jon come after you."

Laurie felt her mouth quirk up in the beginnings of a smile. Maybe it wouldn't be so awful to be a Clucker, just for a little while. She wouldn't have to wear the official Tuckernuck Cluckers shirt every day, right?

After all, the newspapers all said the school was probably closing, so she'd be leaving Ponch and Jon and that stupid Bud Wallace in the dust in no time.

Bud Wallace cleared his throat as he scraped the burned parts off the pan from dinner. "So, we got our classroom assignments today." His dad seemed pretty into the papers he'd taken out of his briefcase, so Bud was hoping this was the perfect time to talk to him. If he was lucky, his dad would hardly hear what he was saying.

Mr. Wallace looked up from his papers. "Assignments?"

So luck had never really been on Bud's side.

He smiled. "You know, office liaison, birthday officer, that kind of thing. It's just a thing they do."

Mr. Wallace got up and clapped Bud on the shoulder. "That's great! So what are you . . . office liaison?"

Bud concentrated on the bowl. He didn't want to look at his dad's face. "Not quite."

"Are you in charge of audiovisuals? Did I tell you I was president of the AV club in high school?" Bud knew all about the AV club and how cool it used to be. Somehow he didn't think his dad was going to think Ponch and Jon were that cool.

"Gerbil Monitor. I'm Gerbil Monitor."

"Gerbil?" Mr. Wallace took off his glasses and wiped them with his pocket square.

"It's a little animal. Like a hamster, but with a tail."

"Oh." Mr. Wallace put his glasses back on. "Well, gerbils are good too." He smiled at Bud.

"Yeah." Bud tried to smile back. His dad didn't have to say anything. Bud could tell how disappointed he was from the way he picked his papers back up. Gerbil duty was the lowest of the low.

Bud attacked the pan with the scrub brush. First day of school, and he was already screwing up. Well, that settled it. He wasn't going to let Ponch and Jon and that Laurie Madison drag him down.

Letter from Mrs. Olivia Hutchins to Bud Wallace

Dear Mr. Wallace:

I am very sorry to hear that you are unhappy with your current classroom duty assignment. Unfortunately, changes cannot be made at this time. If at the end of the semester you still wish to be reassigned, please see me.

Happy monitoring!

Mrs. Olivia Hutchins

> ## Ponch and Jon Care Schedule
> ## from Mrs. Olivia Hutchins
>
> *Bud, Laurie, feel free to arrange the*
> *schedule as you see fit. The important*
> *thing is that all of these things are*
> *done each week.*
>
> Every day: Feeding and fresh water.
> Twice a week: Chew toy and playtime.
> Once a week: Clean cage.

"Chew toy and playtime, Kimmy. Playtime. What am I supposed to do? I can't do playtime with those gerbils," Laurie hissed into the phone desperately. After the bell rang, she'd made what she hoped was a discreet dash behind Mrs. Hutchins's freestanding blackboard, but it wasn't like she could go unnoticed for long. "What kind of lame school has classroom gerbils in sixth grade anyway? What, do they think we're babies?"

"I don't get it. You totally loved Suzy-Q," Kimmy said.

Suzy-Q may have started life as a gerbil, but once Kimmy switched her to an all-sunflower-seed diet, she basically turned into a tennis ball with feet. Not the same thing.

"You know how Suzy-Q went after sunflower seeds? Well, that's how Ponch and Jon are with human flesh."

"Wow, that really stinks. Oh! Did I tell you what happened with my sneakers?" Kimmy didn't seem to be grasping how dire the situation was. Who cared about sneakers?

"Kimmy, what do I do?" Laurie peeked out from behind the blackboard. Bud had wandered over to the gerbil cage and was shooting her periodic glances. He was totally on to her.

"Beats me. I'm really sorry about the hamster thing. Maybe they'll die." Kimmy didn't sound nearly sympathetic enough. "So anyway, this girl, Alyssa?"

"Gerbils."

"What?"

"Gerbils. They're gerbils, not hamsters."

"Right, gerbils, same difference. So at lunch? This girl Alyssa stepped on my sneaker, and it was totally on purpose."

No, Laurie thought, huge difference. Ponch and Jon were gross. They were evil. They weren't cute and fluffy, and they didn't sing and dance on the internet. The two were in no way the same.

"I mean, deliberately, can you believe that? It scuffed!"
Bud had given up all pretense of watching the gerbils and was openly staring at the blackboard. Laurie was totally busted.

"Kimmy, gotta go," she said, cutting Kimmy off in the middle of the smudged sneaker saga, which, honestly, Laurie didn't consider an appropriate topic for a time of crisis (or ever). Kimmy obviously didn't know a thing about gerbils.

Know Your Rodents: A Study Guide for
Kimmy Baranski
by Laurie Madison, grade six

Size: Small, fluffy, and fat.

Tail: Nonexistent.

Activity level: High at night, low in day.

Color: Gold.

Cute?: Yes (especially when wearing a bow, hat, or other accessory).

Verdict: Hamster.

Suggested response: Detached affection.

Size: Small and wiry.

Tail: Long and plumey.

> Activity level: Abnormally high.
> Color: Brown or black.
> Cute?: Definitely not (even with bow or hat).
> Verdict: Gerbil, aka Demon Spawn of Satan.
> Suggested Response: Nuclear.

Bud pointed to the blackboard as Laurie sauntered over nonchalantly. "What was that all about?"

"What?" Laurie shot Bud a cool and unconcerned look. "What do you mean?"

"That whole hiding deal. What was with that?" Bud rubbed his nose in irritation. It made a little wrinkle on top that made him look like he had a snout.

An eighth grader who worked in the school office appeared in the doorway with a note in his hand. He gave Laurie and Bud the once-over before handing the note to Mrs. Hutchins. From the face he made, it didn't look like they passed muster. Laurie blamed the snout.

The eighth grader left, but snouty Bud was still staring at Laurie for an explanation. She shrugged. People probably ducked behind blackboards for secret phone conversations all the time. It was no big deal. If Bud didn't understand that she needed a couple of minutes of private time, that was his tough luck.

Mrs. Hutchins bustled over just in time to save Laurie from coming up with a snappy reply. She looked worried.

"I'm so sorry, kids, but I've got to go up to the office for a little bit. I hate to leave you guys on your first day. . . ."

"We'll be fine, Mrs. Hutchins," Bud said. "No problem at all." Laurie wondered if Bud had somehow missed hearing about Ponch and Jon's last victim. It would explain a lot.

Mrs. Hutchins gave them a relieved smile. "You know where I am if you run into trouble. But I can't imagine you'll have problems." She patted them each on the arm and then hurried out of the room.

Note from Betty Abernathy to Olivia Hutchins

Dear Olivia:

I've compiled the Tutweiler papers you requested—we have documents from her time in Paris a few years before the renovation of the school up through her resignation as principal. They're in the back room of the office.

I know you're looking for a way to save the school, but I don't think you're going to find

it here. I did see the names of some of the
artists and architects you asked about, but
I don't know that there's any connection to
the school there.

Unfortunately, due to the historic nature
of the documents, we can't allow them to
leave the office.

Best,

Betty

P.S. One interesting thing to note. You will
see from the papers that there is no love lost
between Maria Tutweiler and school board
member Wayne LeFranco. That very same
Wayne LeFranco is related to our current
school board president, Walker LeFranco. So
if you're hoping for a sympathetic ear there,
I'm afraid you won't get one.

Bud thrust a grubby-looking gerbil play ball into Laurie's
hands. "Go for it."

Laurie shook her head. "No way." She braced herself
for an argument, but weirdly enough, it didn't come.

Bud just looked down at Ponch and Jon, who were standing up against the aquarium walls watching them, their jaws dripping with venom. He looked doubtful.

"Okay, well, maybe we ease into it? Let them get used to us before we try playtime? I'll change their water and you change their food."

Laurie nodded. She could handle food. How hard could food be? And by the time she filled the dish, Bud probably would've bonded with the suckers, and she wouldn't have to get involved with playtime at all. Or he would've been attacked and killed, at which point she'd need to go the office for help anyway.

Bud carefully took the lid off of the top of the aquarium and put it on the table. Ponch and Jon didn't move—they just watched the whole procedure with interest. Then he lifted out the water bottle and headed to the sink.

Laurie scowled to herself. Ponch and Jon stood watching her expectantly, flexing their knees and rubbing their tiny hands together. She knew they were up to something. She just needed to distract them long enough to grab the dish.

Laurie scanned the room for ideas. A glint by one of the desks caught her eye. There was a button on the floor. Sure, it was big and silver and probably toxic to small rodents. But chances were good they hadn't ever seen anything like it before, so it would be just the thing to boggle their tiny minds. Plus it was shiny, and everybody knows animals go crazy for shiny things. Laurie scooped up the button and dusted it off. She held it up just long enough for Ponch and Jon to fixate on it, and then flipped it into the aquarium. It bounced against the far wall and landed in a pile of cedar chips in the corner.

Ponch and Jon immediately raced over to it, trying to figure out what the amazing shiny thing was. Laurie gave a little internal cheer, took a deep breath, stuck her arm into the cage, and successfully grabbed the food dish. She didn't know what she'd been so worried about. Gerbils were no big deal anyway. Puny little dimwits, that's what they were.

Unfortunately, they were also puny little dimwits with powerful jumping muscles. Laurie had barely taken hold of the bowl when Ponch (or Jon) saw his chance. Turning away from the button, he crouched and gave an enormous leap, landing squarely on Laurie's arm. In one smooth motion, Ponch (or Jon) grabbed hold of her sleeve and shimmied up toward her shoulder. It was like he was a stunt gerbil in an action movie, that's how slick his moves were.

"AAERRERRREGHHHH!!" Laurie shrieked, jerking her arm back and flinging gerbil food all over the room. "GUUUUHRREAAEEEEAAAA!!"

"What the heck?" Bud looked up from the sink just in time to see Ponch (or Jon) go flying across the room and land on one of the pillows in the reading nook. A fine scattering of birdseed and sunflower seeds pattered softly as it hit the ground.

"Laurie, what are you doing?" he yelled, dropping the bottle with a loud thunk.

Laurie shuddered convulsively and rubbed at her arm, trying to get rid of the feeling of tiny claws. "He went after me!" she wailed.

Jon (or Ponch) abandoned the shiny button he was clutching and watched the two of them with interest. He was no dummy. With Bud and Laurie distracted, he knew it was time to make his move. He leaped up and grabbed the edge of the aquarium, pulling himself up onto the rim.

"Aaaah!" Laurie jumped back like she had springs on her feet. "They're after me!"

She grabbed the aquarium lid, pushed Jon (or Ponch)

back inside before he was able to make the jump from the aquarium to her shirt front, and slammed the lid down hard. Jon (or Ponch) went back to his button, cursing loudly.

"Get a grip, Laurie, they're gerbils!" Bud said, rolling his eyes. "Come on, we've got to catch that one."

He made a move toward the tiny escapee on the pillow. But Ponch (or Jon) wasn't giving up that easily. He hissed at Bud in a very non-gerbil-like way, turned tail, and raced out of the room and down the hall.

Bud and Laurie stared at each other in horror.

"He'll kill half the school!" Laurie gasped.

"Mrs. Hutchins will kill us!" Bud groaned. "We'll fail sixth grade!"

Without another word the two took off running down the hallway. There was no way they could let that gerbil escape. But Ponch (or Jon, but for some reason Laurie had decided it was definitely Ponch) was a gerbil on a mission. He could really move. They didn't catch up to him until the main entryway, when he was momentarily distracted by a stepped-on piece of banana.

"Shh." Bud put a finger to his mouth and jerked his head to the left. Then he headed off to Ponch's right.

Laurie nodded in understanding and started slinking

to the left. Once they surrounded that psychotic rodent, he wouldn't have a chance. They'd catch that sucker if they had to squish him to do it.

Theoretically, their plan was terrific. Theoretically, they should've surrounded Ponch and grabbed him easily. Unfortunately, in practice the plan left a lot to be desired.

Bud nodded solemnly at Laurie to let her know he was going in for the grab. But Laurie took the nod to mean that she should make her move. The result was that Laurie and Bud charged at the same time, colliding seconds after Ponch looked up, squealed in horror, and took off toward the auditorium. Laurie didn't even notice—she was too busy careening off of Bud's shoulder and hitting her shin against a potted plant. Bud rebounded in the opposite direction and skittered halfway across the hallway, struggling the whole time to stay on his feet.

He came to a stop right next to Ponch, whose dash for freedom had gotten interrupted when he noticed a terrific-smelling piece of paper smeared with something repulsive. It was amazing how much the entryway had dulled his killer instinct.

Bud smirked smugly at Laurie, swooped down, and scooped Ponch up with one hand. Then he promptly slipped, slamming into the portrait of Hilda the chicken. Which immediately fell off the wall and smashed onto the floor. Breaking the frame.

> ## Split-Second Art Appraisal
> ## by Laurie Madison, grade six
> Subject: Ancient chicken portrait known as Hilda.
> Value: Unknown. Ugly as sin, so how much could it be worth? Possible sentimental value.
> Punishment for destruction: Expulsion? Suspension?
> Verdict: Don't get caught.

Bud and Laurie froze and gaped at Hilda's portrait lying smashed on the floor. Even Ponch took a moment to look horrified before attempting to gnaw a path to freedom through the center of Bud's palm.

When the door to the school office didn't immediately fly open, Laurie figured they had a shot at escaping.

"Pick it up!" she hissed, rushing over to the painting and grabbing one side. "Fix it, quick." It was a lot heavier than it looked. Bud grabbed the other side of the painting and tried to pick it up, but he was severely hampered by the struggling gerbil in his other hand. As far as Laurie was concerned, Ponch should be counting his lucky stars he hadn't ended up as a grease spot on the floor, instead of cussing Bud out and shaking his little fists.

Laurie crouched down and inspected the corner that had hit the ground while Bud adjusted his grip. "Oh, man, it's busted," she said. "A piece here just snapped or something, and the backing paper's got a rip." She smoothed the ripped paper tentatively, trying to figure out how much the damage would show, but just made it worse. The rip flapped back up ominously. "We're never going to get this to stick back down," Laurie said, poking at the hole with her finger.

A piece of the frame came off in her hand. "Oh, man," she said, looking up at Bud. "You totally ruined it!" she said accusingly.

Laurie was expecting an argument or guilty sobbing or something. But Bud didn't look worried or guilty. He looked confused. "Laurie, what the heck?" He pointed at the piece of wood in her hand.

Laurie held up the piece of frame to inspect it. It wasn't a broken shard of wood. It was smooth and polished, and shaped like a perfect letter D. "Huh?" Laurie looked at the frame again. "It's like it's supposed to come out. That's really weird, right?" Laurie ran her finger along the D-shaped hole in the frame. Something caught against her finger. Laurie pulled at it and it came away in her hand easily. It was a piece of paper, rolled into a tiny tight scroll.

"It's a note," Bud said, his eyes getting wider. "Laurie, you don't think . . ."

Laurie carefully unrolled the piece of thin, yellowing paper and looked up at Bud. "Holy cow, Bud," she breathed. "It's a clue. We've found the treasure."

PART TWO

THE FIRST CLUE

**What to Do When You've Unexpectedly
Found a Clue Leading to Untold Riches
(A Chest of Jewels, or Maybe Solid Gold Bars)
by Laurie Madison, grade six**

1. Immediately hide the evidence.
2. Clean up the scene so no one knows what you found.
3. Remount the picture immediately, hoping no one looks at the dumb chicken closely enough to notice the busted edge.
4. Look innocent when your teacher comes out of the office, even if that means coming clean about the flight of the gerbil.
5. Examine the evidence later (in private).

"I'm just so glad he's safe!"

Laurie and Bud had just gotten the painting back up when Mrs. Hutchins came out of the office to investigate the noises. Not very reassuring that it took her so long to investigate, Laurie privately thought. Doesn't make you feel warm and fuzzy about your safety. For the time being, though, she was just happy that Mrs. Hutchins was too caught up in her gerbil buddy to notice that the Hilda the chicken painting was decidedly crooked.

Calliope Judkin had come out of the office with Mrs. Hutchins, though, and she was staring fixedly at the painting. Laurie shifted uncomfortably and forced herself not to look at the frame. Calliope hadn't noticed anything, right?

"Good work, you two. Jon, you've been such a bad boy!" Mrs. Hutchins scolded the crabby gerbil as she hurried off down the hall toward the classroom. So that was Jon, not Ponch after all. Laurie filed that away for future reference, not that she'd be able to tell the evil duo apart later on anyway. "We're just lucky Principal Winkle didn't see you. He's got a real phobia about gerbils," Mrs. Hutchins confided. Then she looked pained. "Scratch that. I didn't say that, okay?"

"Right. Principal Winkle isn't afraid of gerbils. Got it. We didn't hear a thing," Bud agreed.

Mrs. Hutchins nodded at him, but she didn't look like she felt any better.

Laurie glanced back down the hallway. Calliope was still standing in the school entryway, looking thoughtful. Coincidence, Laurie thought. It must be. She shot Bud a look to see if he'd noticed Calliope, but he'd switched into brownnosing mode.

"We'd better get this little cutie back to his home. I'm

sure Ponch is missing him." Bud smiled. Laurie thought he was overdoing the suck-up routine a little. Cutie? It was a stretch to call Jon cute any day, but especially since two minutes ago he'd been doing his best to sink his teeth into the fleshy parts between Bud's fingers.

If Ponch was missing Jon, though, he had a funny way of showing it. By the time they got back, he'd shifted every bit of cedar to the right side of the aquarium and was sitting on the glass bottom, trembling with rage. Mrs. Hutchins didn't look fazed, though. With no protective gear or evasive maneuvers or anything, she took off the lid of the aquarium, just like it was no big deal. Then she plunked Jon down inside and patted him on the head. With no shedding of blood whatsoever.

Laurie had to admit she was impressed. But the only thing she could concentrate on was the tiny scroll clenched in the palm of her hand. It was all she could do not to make up some excuse and run out.

"Didn't expect to have such an exciting first day as a monitor, did you?" Mrs. Hutchins smiled.

"Nope. Sure didn't. You can say that again," Laurie enthused.

Bud glared at her. "It was exciting, that's for sure."

"That's it for today, then. See you tomorrow!" Mrs.

Hutchins gave the gerbil cage a loving pat and headed back to her desk.

Laurie packed her book bag at super-slow speeds. That piece of paper was hers—there was no way Bud was getting his grubby paws on it. If she moved at a glacial pace, Bud would have no choice but to leave before her. Then she could make her escape.

Bud, however, had a plan of his own. He was waiting for her as she rounded the corner into the main entryway.

"So?" he demanded, stepping in front of Laurie as she tried to scoot down the hallway. "Let's look at it. What does it say?"

Laurie tried to brush past him. But it's not easy to brush past someone almost twice your size. (Not that he really was twice her size, but Laurie felt like he was.)

"I found it too, Laurie, it's not yours." Bud was on the edge of whiny.

Laurie stopped and folded her arms. "Sorry, Bud. No dice. I found it, okay? All you did was act like a klutz. This paper means treasure, and sorry, I'm not giving it up."

Bud gave a short barky laugh that freaked Laurie out. "Treasure? Is that what you care about? Whoever solves that puzzle can write his own ticket, Laurie. Maybe even give the speech at eighth-grade graduation. Can you imagine how awesome that would be?"

Laurie stared at Bud like he was an alien who had just sprouted an extra nose and waggled his antennae at her. She had a very difficult time imagining how awesome it would be to give the speech at eighth-grade graduation. In fact, the word awesome didn't appear anywhere in Laurie's assessment of that scenario.

"Seriously, Bud? Eighth-grade graduation? That's what you care about?" Bud was even weirder than she'd thought. Eighth-grade graduation wasn't for another two years, and everybody knew the school was going to be closed down by then.

"Don't you?" Bud's eyes goggled slightly. "I mean, sure, treasure, that's great, but the speech? You can't buy that, Laurie. It's an honor."

Laurie stared at Bud for a long second. He wasn't fooling around—he was really serious. It was weird. Weird enough to make her think about changing her plans.

"Besides." Bud shrugged. "If you don't, I could always just go tell Mrs. Hutchins what we found."

Laurie bit her lip. There was no way Bud Wallace was taking this away from her.

"Okay," Laurie started slowly. "How about this? We both read the note and go get the treasure. We share the glory—I get the treasure, and you get eighth-grade graduation. But until we've got that treasure in our hands, we tell no one, okay? Not our parents, not our friends, not Calliope Judkin, got it?"

"Calliope Judkin?" Bud looked confused. Laurie didn't bother to fill him in.

"Is that a deal?" Laurie demanded. She didn't think it was much to ask, really. They'd probably only need to keep quiet for a day or two. They'd have the treasure by the weekend at the latest. By the time Bud realized he wasn't getting his eighth-grade graduation glory, she'd be long gone with the gold bars and jewels.

Bud nodded. "Deal." He was already mentally writing his eighth-grade graduation speech. His dad was going to be so psyched.

"Okay then." Laurie grabbed Bud by the arm and dragged him outside and down the front steps, past the weird carved stone sculpture Maria Tutweiler had put in the yard outside the school.

Before the school was Tuckernuck Hall Intermediate, it had been the ancestral home of the Tutweiler family. And when Maria Tutweiler had turned the old Victorian house into a school, she apparently didn't care about things like "clashing" or "good taste." So even though they'd fixed it all up with classrooms, a gym, and a weird round bell tower, there were lots of non-school-like features, like elaborately carved arches over some of the doorways, a big picture of Mark Twain made out of wire in the library, dark patterned wood floors, and even some stained-glass windows here and there. Not to mention the mangy chicken portrait.

The total effect was one big mishmash, with art deco and more modern sections mixed right in with the old Victorian sections. The Cluckers all thought it came together and worked, but people like School Board President Walker LeFranco just thought it proved how crazy Maria Tutweiler was.

But most important for Laurie, the fact that it used to be a real house meant that there was an old gardening supply area under the porch. And since Jack thought that every incoming Clucker should know about at least one secret hiding place, Laurie knew about the hidden supply nook. Glancing around to make sure there was no one watching, Laurie shoved Bud into the cramped space.

Laurie pushed aside the ancient gardening imple-ments, unclenched her fist, and slowly unrolled the (now slightly damp) scroll.

"Well," she said. "Here goes nothing."

CONGRATULATIONS, clever Tuckernuckers! Maria Tutweiler is no match for you, my friends. Well-read youngsters like you know that, as Miss Emily Dickinson said, "Hope is the thing with Feathers." And so is our chicken friend, Hilda, the thing with feathers. So bravo, young poetry aficionados. Well done.

Now it is time for you to make a choice. You can continue on and follow my clues wherever they may lead, or you may remain here, where you started. The choice is entirely yours. If you choose to continue on with my clues, prepare yourselves, for it will be a challenging journey. Choose wisely, and continue on to the next page.

Happy sleuthing!

Maria Tutweiler

"What the heck?" Bud was tired of reading over Laurie's shoulder. He reached out and took the paper, shaking his head. "What the heck is that about the chicken? Hilda's a thing with feathers? Of course she's a thing with feathers."

The light was dawning in Laurie's mind, though. "Shoot, I get it! And we just studied that last year too. Man, I'm such a dork. It's the poem!"

"What is?" Bud always thought of himself as more of a science-type guy.

"That line, 'Hope is the thing with feathers.' It's the first line in a poem by Emily Dickinson. I *knew* it was something about Hope. I can't believe I thought it was a stupid person's name."

"Yeah, well, if I'd just studied the poem, I would've gotten it too. Probably wouldn't have just accidentally stumbled onto it either. Geez, it's simple," Bud boasted.

Laurie glared at him. Never mind that nobody had gotten it before now. She was pretty sure that even if Bud had been an Emily Dickinson scholar he wouldn't have solved it. But they were a team now, right? So she gritted her teeth and held her tongue.

"So we're going on to the next page? We're not just staying where we started, right?"

"As if."

Bud carefully separated the pages and turned to the

second one. Squinting, he began to read aloud the spidery handwriting that once belonged to Maria Tutweiler.

Dear Tuckernucker, Brave and True,
   If you are reading this clue, you have demonstrated
your knowledge and interest in things poetic and
sublime, and your undeniable curiosity. Now I
will take this test of your skills one step further.
Remember, to journey on the path of understanding,
you must first know what it is you wish to
understand. Good luck!

Cat! who hast passed thy grand climacteric,
How many mice and rats hast in thy days
Destroyed? How many tit-bits stolen? Gaze
With those bright languid segments green, and prick
Those velvet ears—but prithee do not stick
Thy latent talons in me, and up-raise
Thy gentle mew, and tell me all thy frays
Of fish and mice, and rats and tender chick.
Nay, look not down, nor lick thy dainty wrists—
For all thy wheezy asthma, and for all
Thy tail's tip is nicked off, and though the fists

Of many a maid have given thee many a maul,
Still is that fur as soft as when the lists
In youth thou enteredst on glass-bottled wall.

"Come on, Laurie. What the heck." Bud broke a stick in half and threw half of it at the ground. Apparently not satisfied with the sound it made, he turned and kicked at the wooden porch supports for good measure. "It doesn't even make sense. I mean, look there." Bud jabbed at the paper with the other half of the stick. "Prithee? Is she serious?"

Laurie didn't answer. She didn't have any clue what the stupid poem meant. She hadn't had any ideas the first ten times he'd asked, and she hadn't had any lightbulbs go off in the meantime.

"So we *know* she's crazy now. Totally bonkers. The chicken was one thing, but this? Cats? This is totally insane. There probably isn't even a stupid treasure, it's probably just a weird hoax." Bud kicked the post again, and a piece of gray paint flecked off onto his shoe. One of the reasons given for closing Tuckernuck Hall was that there was no money for upkeep, and the school was sliding into disrepair. Bud seemed to be doing everything he could to help it along its way.

"So did she write this piece of trash? Or is it Dickinson too?"

"It's not Dickinson," Laurie muttered.

"Are you sure?" Bud kicked the post again. "It could be. Maybe Tutweiler really liked her. Maybe she was crazy obsessed."

Laurie shook her head. "It doesn't sound like Dickinson, okay? I don't know who wrote it, Bud. Just give it a rest." Laurie closed her eyes and tried to organize her thoughts.

How Close I Am to Snapping
by Laurie Madison, grade six

1. Close enough that if he says one more word against Maria Tutweiler or Tuckernuck Hall, I'll rip his head off.
2. Or jab him with that pointy stick.
3. Actually, one more word period. About anything.
4. Close enough that it's time for some deep breathing.

Bud kicked the post again, and a big flake of paint landed on Laurie's head. That was all it took. Deep breathing can only fix so much. Laurie snapped.

"That's it!" she said, rolling the scroll back up and slipping it into her jacket pocket. "I'm done. I'm going home. I'll figure it out tomorrow. If you have any huge insights, you can tell me then. But since Maria Tutweiler is addressing her clues to poetry aficionados, it sounds to me like I'm the only one with any chance of figuring it out, Mr. Dur-de-Dur-Is-That-a-Poem?"

Laurie grabbed her book bag and flounced off before Bud even had time to shut his mouth.

Reasons That Horace (Bud) Wallace
Is an Idiot
by Laurie Madison, grade six

1. Totally ruining the architecture of the school with his irritating kicking habit.
2. Hasn't even heard of Emily Dickinson. I mean, come on. Seriously?
3. Okay, maybe he's heard of her, but still woefully ignorant.
4. No help in solving problems, only good at complaining.
5. What's up with that ego anyway? Eighth-grade graduation, my butt.

‒

Laurie plunked down the basket of garlic bread and slumped into her chair at the dining room table. She'd scoured the hallways after she'd ditched Bud and hadn't found a single cat painting, statue, or forgotten litter box. She'd even looked at every stupid carving in the molding of the history wing, and nothing. No cats. It wasn't even worth the glare she'd gotten from Coach Burton in the gym. And she could tell by the gleam in Jack's eye that he was in one of his pick-on-Laurie moods.

Jack managed to keep his mouth shut until Mr. Madison had put down the Parmesan cheese. "So did Laurie tell you?" Jack said through a mouthful of spaghetti. He grinned a tomatoey grin at her. Laurie averted her eyes before she was turned off of spaghetti forever.

"She solved the puzzle."

Laurie went cold. He couldn't know. Could he?

"What?" Mrs. Madison paused mid-Parmesan shake. "Laurie didn't tell me anything. What puzzle? Not THE puzzle?"

"Shut up, Jack." Laurie scowled at the garlic bread like it had committed hideous crimes against garlic bread everywhere. She grabbed the most offensive piece and tore it into pieces on her plate.

"Laurie called me at school the other day to tell me she'd solved the first clue." Jack elbowed Laurie in the arm playfully. She refused to look up. She felt almost limp with relief. He didn't know anything.

Mrs. Madison looked serious. "Now, Laurie, you know you're not supposed to use that cell phone during school hours. It's for emergencies. I don't want to have to go down to the school to get it back from Miss Abernathy if you get caught."

"Aw, come on, Mom, lighten up! She'd figured out the whole 'all you need is Hope' clue. She's got to call for that, right, Laurie?"

"So was it gold bars or a chest full of jewels?" Mr. Madison winked at her across the table. The chest full of jewels/gold bars debate had been raging in the Madison household for years.

Laurie picked up one of the chunks of dismembered garlic bread and gnawed a huge piece off of the end. Somebody was going to pay for this, and if it had to be a defenseless piece of garlic bread, so be it.

Mrs. Madison patted Laurie on the arm. "Never mind them, Laurie. Was it the word Hope? You figured that Hope must be a person, right? That one got me too, when I was your age."

"That one gets everybody," Mr. Madison said. "Too bad it's not right. That seems like a great solution. I still think there must be some Hope lurking somewhere."

Laurie shoveled the rest of her garlic bread into her mouth. It would blow their minds if she told them the truth, and putting Jack in his place would feel pretty awesome. It's not like the agreement with Bud was that big a deal—he'd pretty much forfeited the agreement not to tell with his lousy attitude. But there was no way she was filling them in now. They could just wait and be jealous when she hauled in the loot. Maybe she'd let them visit her at her fabulous vacation house in Hawaii. Maybe. Besides, there was no way she could spill anything with a mouth full of garlic bread. Just call it extra security.

"So there are no people named Hope anywhere with the school? Nowhere?" Laurie said when her mouth was empty and the temptation to spill her guts had passed. She might not tell them anything, but that didn't mean she couldn't pump them for information.

"Not a one," said Mrs. Madison sadly. "But that's a good start, hon. I was at school for a month before that one occurred to me."

"Any cat pictures or statues? Like that ugly Hilda portrait? Except maybe a kitten or something?" Laurie was willing to admit she might have missed something. It's tough to do a thorough search when you know Coach Burton is watching your every move.

"Nooo, I don't think so." Mrs. Madison gave Laurie a speculative look. "Not that I recall. Not when I was there anyway, and I don't think things have really changed. Gary, do you remember anything like that?"

"What, you think Hope's a cat now?"

She shot Jack a look that would curdle milk, but he just shrugged it off.

"Just trying to keep up with the new theories, that's all." He grinned again. Laurie decided maybe she was put off spaghetti after all.

Jack punched Laurie in the arm lightly. "You know I'm just messing with you. You know what? You find that treasure, and I'll do your laundry for a month. No, a *year*. What do you say, Laurie?"

Laurie smiled. "Deal."

Cat Poem Meaning: Ideas
by Horace Wallace Jr.
Thought one: Poem means we should find a particular cat. Probably old and mean.

Physical details probably not exact match to poem.
Thought two: Since clue was left over seventy-five years ago, cat in question is probably dead by now. So look for dead cat.
Thought three: Crud.

Laurie Madison, note to self:
How long do cats live anyway?

"Well, *obviously*, we're not looking for a real cat here," Bud said the next day when he ran across Laurie eating breakfast in the cafeteria.

"OBVIOUSLY." Laurie rolled her eyes. "It would be dumb to think it's a real cat. They only live about twenty years, so any cat Maria Tutweiler would be referring to would be long gone."

"So maybe a cat statue or painting or something? Like a cat version of Hilda?"

"Please, I'm trying to eat here." Laurie made a retching sound. "I didn't find anything like that. I looked."

"Okay, but there's got to be one somewhere. So we should just split up and start looking again? You take the eastern half and I'll take the western?" Bud eyed Laurie warily. He didn't know if the retching sound she'd made was voluntary or involuntary.

"Fine, we'll do another search. We'll have this solved in no time." Laurie was still mad, Bud could tell. She wasn't even meeting his eyes.

Bud stood a moment in silence, watching Laurie chew.

"Take a picture, it'll last longer." Laurie didn't even look up.

"You know," he said tentatively, "I'll bet Maria Tutweiler didn't think it was going to take longer than twenty years to solve this thing. She probably thought it would only take a couple of months."

Laurie didn't say anything. She just frowned a little and continued chewing. Bud figured that must be one chewy biscuit. She didn't seem to be catching his drift.

"She probably didn't think a real cat would have time to die, see what I mean?" Bud tried again.

"I know." Laurie finally looked up, but only to glare at him.

Bud finished his word problems and put down his pencil. "Done."

Mr. Wallace clicked the stopwatch and smiled at him. "Plenty of time left. Good job, Bud." He pulled the paper over. "Assuming they're right, that is." Mr. Wallace punched Bud playfully on the shoulder.

Bud cleared his throat. "So, you know, at school, there's supposed to be this treasure."

Mr. Wallace checked off his word problems one by one. "What's that?"

"A treasure. It's supposed to be hidden somewhere in the school. With clues. The old principal put them out so a kid would find it."

"That sounds fun." Mr. Wallace made an X on the paper. "You missed number four, Bud." He pushed the paper back. "You're not going to get into the Ivy League with work like that. Can you see where you went wrong?"

Bud looked at the paper and went over the problem in his head. Shoot. He'd forgotten to carry the one. "Sorry, Dad," he said, fixing it.

Mr. Wallace took the paper back and smiled. "I knew you knew how to do it."

"So the treasure, at school. Everybody's been trying to find it, for, like, fifty years. But no one can solve the first clue, right? It's a total mystery."

Mr. Wallace frowned. "This isn't a true story, is it? It's some kind of school legend?"

Bud shrugged. "Well, no, see . . ." Bud tried to figure out a way to explain. Bud's dad had gone to Hamilton. It would've been so much easier if his mom had been there. She'd been a Clucker.

"Sort of a legend, I guess." Bud stared at the red X on his paper.

Mr. Wallace looked at Bud for a long minute. "Hamilton didn't have anything like that. And your mother . . ." Mr. Wallace took off his glasses and rubbed his eyes. "Your mother never mentioned treasure to me."

Bud could've kicked himself. He hadn't meant to make his dad sad again. "It's just a crazy story." Bud shifted in his chair. He should've just stuck to the word problems.

Bud cleared his throat. "Can I use the computer to work on my homework?"

Mr. Wallace took his hand away from his eyes and gave Bud a weak smile. "Sure thing, kid."

Bud got up and headed to the study. He wouldn't mention the treasure again. Not until he'd found it.

━━

Laurie was watching Misti Pinkerton pry the metallic lid off a container of yogurt when the crackly announcement started over the ancient PA system. Laurie hardly noticed. Odds were pretty good Misti was going to end up wearing a good portion of that yogurt before lunch was over. Misti was what you could call spill prone.

It was hard to ignore Principal Winkle's cheery voice though. Especially since he was practically shouting.

"Good morning, Cluckers! This is your princi"PAL," Martin Winkle! Today's the big day, so put on your Clucker hats. It's time for the first Clucker rally of the year. Warm up your vocal cords, because we'll be expecting some beautiful harmonies this afternoon!"

The PA system squealed with feedback and then shut off. Laurie felt sick.

"There's not really a Clucker hat, right? That's just a figure of speech?" Laurie's mom had every bit of Clucker merchandise there was, including the limited-edition clucking cookie jar, but she'd never seen a hat. Laurie really hoped it wasn't some new thing. She wasn't a fashion plate or anything, but even she knew that a chicken hat would be a hard look to pull off.

Misti's face brightened. "You mean like the shirt? I hope so. Maybe they'll give them out at the rally."

"Great." Laurie scooched back a little as Misti's lid came off, spraying Misti with a fine yogurt mist. Not bad, considering Misti's history. Yesterday she'd spent the afternoon with a stripe of Thousand Island dressing down her front.

Laurie watched as Misti licked the yogurt lid before setting it aside. She'd been hanging out with Misti and Kimmy since second grade, but in all that time, she'd never really noticed Misti was so . . . well, Misti-like. Maybe it just hadn't been so obvious when Kimmy was around.

"Yeah, so I figured it all out." Bud jerked the chair next to Laurie out from the table and threw himself into it cockily.

Misti stopped, spoonful of plain yogurt still in her mouth, and glared at Bud. "Excuse me, Laurie, but I'd better go before my sweet tooth offends someone." Misti put the not-quite-clean spoon into her bag, gathered her things together quickly, and huffed off.

"Man." Bud looked deflated. "People just won't let that go."

"What, we eat together now? I don't think we're at the eating together stage, okay?" Laurie looked around nervously. It was hard not to notice the nasty looks being thrown in their direction.

Bud barely paid attention. "It was just one science project. Man, I wish I'd done photosynthesis."

Laurie shrugged. She didn't really know what to say. "That might've been better."

Bud gave her a half grin. "You know the stupidest part? I was just so psyched that my dad thought my presentation was good enough to take to the school board. I was all for it. I wasn't thinking about what would happen if we won."

Laurie crumpled up her bag. "Misti hates plain yogurt. It makes her cranky. I hear there's an underground sugar network in high school, though, so people should forgive you then."

Bud sighed heavily. "Yeah, well, I figured it out. If anyone cares."

Laurie looked skeptical. "What, the clue? And how'd you do that? There are no freaking cats in the whole school. What'd you do? Find a dead cat?"

Bud blushed furiously. "She said it right there—we have to know what we're trying to understand. And we didn't. Get it?"

Laurie tried to look like she knew what he was talking about, but she didn't have a clue. "Okay, fine, what's that supposed to mean?" Who cared what Bud Wallace thought, anyway?

"That poem. She left off the title, right? So that's the

clue. We need to know the title to solve the clue. It's a poem by Keats, and it's called 'Mrs. Reynolds' Cat.' So there. Clue solved."

Laurie felt her skepticism waning. "So how'd you find that out?" It sounded good, she had to admit. She couldn't believe she hadn't even considered the name of the poem.

"Just a little thing I like to call Google," Bud bragged. He seemed to have recovered from the whole Misti snub. "I just typed in that first line, and the work was done."

He opened his backpack and pulled out a page printed off of the internet. It was an exact copy of the poem in the scroll, except Bud was right. Right there along the top, it said "Mrs. Reynolds' Cat" by John Keats.

Laurie nodded. "Wow. Good job, Einstein. You're right." It was some impressive Googling.

Bud stopped smirking and broke into a genuine smile. "No problem."

Laurie wasn't willing to let him off the hook though. "So Mrs. Reynolds' cat *what*? Or is Keats the important part? I still don't see how that leads us anywhere except to a big old dead end."

"Well, whatever." Bud slumped back into the chair. "It's something, though."

Laurie nodded. "Yeah, it's something."

They sat in silence for a second, staring at the poem. Finally Bud cleared his throat.

"It must be Keats, right? Maybe something in the English department?"

"Laurie!" Misti came racing over before Laurie could respond. "Oh, hello, Bud." Her voice was so icy Laurie's milk almost froze over. But Misti was too excited to keep up the pose for long.

"Laurie, you were right! We get hats!" She put on a baseball hat with a big chicken face on the front, wings on the sides, and scrawny yellow legs dangling down the back. "Aren't they great? This school is the best!"

Laurie put her head on her arms and groaned.

———

"Okay, kids! Let's hear it for Tuckernuck Hall!" Principal Winkle looked out over the sea of bobbing Clucker hats and smiled. It was amazing—give a kid some Clucker gear, teach them the fight song, and *poof*—instant school spirit. It never failed.

Principal Winkle nodded to Mr. Murphy, the band director. The older students erupted in cheers at the opening notes of the Tuckernuck Hall fight song.

This last semester was going to be a good one.

Clucker Fight Song

Remember—sing out with spirit and enthusiasm!
(Clapping encouraged!)

All Tuckernuck Cluckers should give a cheer
Because us Cluckers do not bow to fear.
We're gonna win win win the game today.
We'll use our pluck and brains whatever come
what may.
And we will peck! peck! peck! at every foe.
We'll show our opposition where to go,
And we will crow our victory out loud.
Oh , and how! CLUCK! CLUCK! CLUCK!
YAY!

"Wasn't that awesome, Laurie?" Misti skipped along-side Laurie, her hat's chicken legs flapping out behind her. "This is the best school. We never had assemblies like that last year!"

Laurie felt a pang of guilt. She was the worst Clucker ever. She stopped skipping, tearing off her Clucker hat and dragging it behind her by one spindly yellow leg. This was going to be a bad, bad year. Without Kimmy around, everything was wrong. Misti was all weird and chicken crazed, and the whole Clucker thing just seemed stupid. Besides, she wasn't even going to be a Clucker. She'd stick around until she found that treasure, maybe, but after that she'd do whatever it took to be a Hamilton Hornet. But she wasn't about to say that to a girl in a chicken hat.

Misti, still skipping, linked arms with Crystal Martin. She didn't even notice as Laurie dropped behind and then ducked into an alcove near the auditorium doors.

Bud wandered out of the auditorium, humming the "peck! peck! peck!" part of the song under his breath. He didn't spot Laurie until she'd grabbed him by the upper arm and dragged him into the doorway next to the auditorium.

"Wha—?" Bud pulled his arm away. "I bruise easily, okay? Watch it."

"Sorry, Princess. We need to find out about Keats. Singing time is over." Laurie didn't want to waste any more time. She needed solid gold bars, and she needed them now.

Bud made a face at the princess line, but he didn't argue. Being the ruling Clucker was looking pretty appealing. Maybe he'd get a bigger hat.

"I can't miss class, Laurie," Bud said, checking his watch nervously.

Laurie rolled her eyes at him. "We have plenty of time. I know a shortcut—we'll just do a quick sweep of the English hall, find the Keats painting or statue or whatever, and then we'll be golden."

"Well, okay. But fast." Bud wasn't about to be late the first week of school.

Laurie grabbed Bud by the arm and raced off down the hallway. Without hesitation, she dashed around the corner, down a narrow passageway and came out in the English hall. Or what she thought was the English hall.

Tipoffs That You're Not in an English Hallway, but in a Deceptively Similar Music Hallway by Laurie Madison, grade six

1. Music stands in corner.
2. Bulletin board decorated with pictures of Beethoven and music notes.
3. The presence of Trinity Harbaugh, music geek extraordinaire.
4. Singing cherubs painted above the doorways. (Seriously, what's that about?)

> 5. Sheet music on floor instead of regular notebook paper.
> 6. Actual music being played. Go figure.

"Shoot." Laurie looked at the music stand perched outside a classroom doubtfully. "That doesn't look right."

"Oh, man!" Bud looked at his watch again. "Where are we? Thanks a lot, Laurie. We're gonna get tardies!"

Laurie waved her hand at him dismissively. "It's fine, it's just through . . . here." She picked a door at random and darted through. Which was a mistake.

"Can I help you?" There was a teacher at the desk in the front of the empty classroom, maybe in a planning period. She closed her grade book and looked up just as Laurie skittered to a halt and Bud slammed into her.

"No. Uh. Sorry." Laurie had barely gotten the words out before she'd turned and hurried out, leaving Bud alone in the doorway.

"We . . . uh. Didn't know anyone would be here." Bud felt weird about just running out like that. But he didn't know what he was supposed to say either. He wished the teacher would stop staring at him.

"Are you here to sign up for the choral auditions?" The teacher stood up, smoothed her skirt, and pointed to an audition sheet near the door. Bud eyed it nervously. Choral auditions were not his thing.

"No, really, just a mistake." He gave a half smile. Why wouldn't she just go back to her grade book?

"Because you sound to me like a tenor. Are you a tenor?" The teacher was getting closer. Bud knew he had to get out, and fast. But for some reason, his feet weren't listening to him.

"No, not a tenor." At least he didn't think so. Bud wasn't entirely sure what he was.

"Because we need tenors. And I believe you're mistaken. I think you're a tenor."

Bud swallowed noisily. The teacher gave him an encouraging smile. "Don't be shy. The auditions aren't for a while. You have time to prepare." She held out a pen. It was so close, he could almost touch it. All he had to do was sign his name, and she'd be happy. It was tempting. But then Bud thought about what his dad would say.

"No, I don't want to audition! Sorry!" Bud's feet finally got the message and turned and hurried out. He hated to be rude like that, but he had no choice. He knew one thing, though. He could never come back to the music hall again. Ever.

Laurie was bouncing on the balls of her feet at the end

of the hallway. "What happened to you?" she hissed. "Did she bust you? Give you detention? What happened in there?"

Bud rolled his eyes at her. "Forget it, okay? Nothing happened." He took off running down the hallway, his heavy footsteps echoing through the empty halls. The last thing he needed was a tardy the first week of school. His dad had enough stuff to worry about without Bud screwing up. That teacher was the least of his problems.

TARDY WARNING FOR

Horace Wallace Jr.

MR. WALLACE,

This is to notify you that you have used your ONE (1) tardy warning for this semester. All subsequent tardies will be referred to the office and noted on your permanent record.

You have been warned.

Sincerely,

MR. MARSHALL DEAL

Sixth-grade science

"It was a mistake, okay? I took a wrong turn." Laurie tried to keep her temper under control as she finished filling Ponch and Jon's food dish. Bud just frowned at her and attached the water bottle in silence.

It's not like Bud had even gotten a tardy; it was just a tardy warning. He was lucky Mr. Deal gave out warnings. Mrs. Humphries had just given her a flat-out tardy. If she didn't watch it, she'd be explaining herself in front of Principal Winkle before long. But that wasn't something she was going to think about now.

"There's got to be stuff about Keats there. Something noticeable. A painting or something." Laurie scowled at Ponch (or Jon), who was attacking a sunflower seed and looking at her in a threatening way. She wasn't scared of him. Well, not now that she'd figured out she could just pour the new food into the bowl from three inches above the aquarium. So it was a little messy, so what?

But Laurie's hopes died when she and Bud made it to the English hall. Without a million kids rushing to class, it looked like the music hall's stodgy twin brother. No painted cherubs, singing or otherwise, no bulletin boards, no paintings, nothing. It even smelled boring.

"So where's the Keats shrine?" Bud asked, giving

Laurie a snarky look. Never mind that the Keats thing was his idea. She needed taking down a peg. Mr. Deal was gunning for him now, and it was all her fault.

"There's got to be something!" Laurie groaned, scanning the walls desperately. "What a lame hallway!"

Bud couldn't help but agree. It was definitely lame.

Suddenly Laurie grabbed Bud by the arm. "Look! By the window!" At the end of the hallway, there was a small nook with a sculpted bust in it.

Bud and Laurie both hurried to be the first one to the nook. Laurie could practically taste the treasure.

"See?" Laurie said, looking at the bust triumphantly. "Right there it says . . . oh, wait."

"Homer." Bud couldn't believe it. "What the heck, Laurie? Why Homer?"

Laurie shook her head. It just didn't make sense. Where was Keats? Shouldn't it be Keats instead?

There had to be a logical explanation, and Laurie wasn't going to wait around for it to fall into her lap. She headed to the nearest classroom and stuck her head in the door. A teacher from the High-Water Pants and Overtucked Shirt School of Fashion was hanging a Globe Theatre poster with a smiley cartoon Shakespeare on his bulletin board.

"Hey!" Laurie barked. "I have an English question."

The teacher looked up hopefully. "Really? You do?"

Laurie nodded and motioned for Bud to come over, but he didn't move. He wasn't about to get involved in another teacher situation, like with the music hall. Not like there were English auditions, but whatever.

"It's about Keats. You know, Keats? He wrote poems?" Laurie said slowly.

"Yes, of course. Go on." The teacher nodded. There was no doubt he knew Keats. It was like his salivary glands had kicked in at the sound of his name.

"So, is there anything Keats-related here? Like maybe a painting? Or anything?"

"Or statue!" Bud called from where he was rooted to the floor.

"Or a statue," Laurie continued. "Maybe something they used to have here? Did it used to be Keats instead of Homer in that nook?" She eyed the teacher warily, like he was a rabid dog.

The teacher smiled at her. "Keats, yes. Yes, of course. What year are you?" It was like he hadn't even heard what she'd asked. Laurie's danger sensors were flashing. She didn't see what that had to do with anything, but she figured it couldn't hurt to answer.

"Sixth."

"Sixth. Yes. So you have . . ."

"Mr. Robinson." Laurie was getting impatient. It didn't seem like a difficult question, but with this guy, who knew? She wished she knew who he was exactly so she could ask Jack about him.

"Robinson, of course. Hmm. Well, we don't usually cover the English Romantic movement in sixth grade, but perhaps we could make an exception. Especially when there's such a strong interest."

"No, it's fine, I don't need to study him. I just need to know if there's a painting? Or statue . . ." Laurie trailed off. She was starting to feel panicked. This was not going well.

Bud was glad he'd kept his distance.

"And I'm not in your class, okay?" Laurie threw out again.

The teacher looked thoughtful. "No painting that I'm aware of, and Homer's always been Homer. But maybe . . . I know! We could have an English Romantics club! Doesn't that sound fun? After school, maybe once a week? We could have snacks!"

He did that stroking-his-beard thing Laurie had always heard about but didn't think people actually did.

It looked creepy as all get out, and Laurie figured it wasn't a good sign. She knew when to cut her losses.

"Yeah, whatever. So no painting? Too bad. Thanks, bye!" Laurie turned and ran. Behind her, the teacher smiled to himself and went back into his classroom. Laurie didn't breathe easy until she was back in the main hallway. She'd have to be careful in the English hall from now on, that was certain. She just hoped he'd forget about the whole club thing.

Notice on the English Hall Bulletin Board

EXCITING NEW CLUB!
By Popular Demand, the English Department
will start the very first
ENGLISH ROMANTIC POETS' CLUB!
All the Byron, Shelley, and Keats
you've asked for.
Meetings, Mondays after school
WITH SNACKS!
Sign up with Mr. Sanchez, room 212.

"Well, that stinks. Total dead end," Bud grumbled. He checked his watch. If he hurried, he could still make the late bus. At least the day wouldn't be a total loss.

"We'll figure it out," Laurie said through gritted teeth as Bud hurried toward the bus line. She wasn't entirely sure she meant it, but it's not like they had any choice. They had to figure it out. How lame would it be to be the first people to find the clues and then hit a dead end on the very first one?

"Hey, Laurie!"

Laurie wheeled around just in time to see Misti hurrying after her. Laurie stifled a groan. Now that Kimmy was out of the picture, Misti seemed to have decided that she and Laurie were BFFs. Laurie wasn't entirely sure how she felt about that.

"I lost my sweater. Do you remember if I had it after assembly?" Misti asked breathlessly. "I can't find it anywhere."

Laurie thought back, but the whole Clucker assembly was something she'd rather not think about. It was all just a blur of feathery hats and chicken dancing anyway.

"Sorry, Misti, I don't remember."

Misti sighed. "That's okay. I probably left it in Reynolds. Fingers crossed!" she said, starting to skip.

Laurie stopped dead in her tracks. "What did you say?"

Misti skipped more slowly. "That I probably left it in

Reynolds? At the assembly?" Misti hesitated as Laurie started bobbing up and down like an apple at Halloween. It was like Laurie had turned into a certified crazy person. "Remember? The assembly in Reynolds Auditorium?"

A huge grin burst across Laurie's face, making Misti's eyes widen even more. Misti took a step back. Laurie's impression of a crazy person was really good.

"Bud!" Laurie shrieked. He jerked his head around in annoyance as he headed down the steps toward the bus. "We're such idiots! Reynolds Auditorium!"

Ten kids in between them caught the crazy vibe Laurie was giving off and made plenty of room as she went racing away. Bud fist punched the air and hurried back inside after her, almost colliding with Calliope Judkin as he ran. They were back in the game.

Plaque outside Reynolds Auditorium

MRS. LUCINDA HAYES REYNOLDS

This auditorium is dedicated to Mrs. Lucinda Hayes Reynolds, in appreciation of her generosity toward Tuckernuck Hall, her selfless dedication to education and the arts, and her friendship and tireless good humor.

"It wasn't Keats, it was Mrs. Reynolds!" Laurie did a miniversion of the Clucker crow.

"Okay, great, she's awesome. Now what? Where is it?" Bud looked around wildly. The students who hadn't caught the crazy vibe from Laurie earlier caught it now and decided the auditorium entryway was not a place to be. Even Laurie thought Bud was looking a wee bit scary. Especially around the eyes.

Laurie leaned against the auditorium doors. "My guess? In there somewhere."

"So what are we waiting for?"

Laurie tugged at the door. It didn't budge. "Locked up tight."

"What? No way!" Bud rattled the door and kept rattling like if he did it long enough the door would just fall off.

Laurie smacked him on the hand. "Cut it out! It's locked. As in, with a key? Which we don't have."

Bud's shoulders slumped. "Shoot. So what, we just wait?"

Laurie shrugged. "I guess, unless you want to break in."

Bud opened his mouth to answer but shut it abruptly when Misti huffed up to Laurie and stopped, arms folded.

"Was it in there?"

Laurie shot Bud a panicky look. "What?" How had Misti found out? Laurie couldn't believe it.

"My sweater. Did you even look?"

"Uh, no. Sorry." Relief washed over Laurie.

Misti's eyes narrowed skeptically. "You're losing it, Laurie. You really are."

Laurie just nodded. No arguing with that.

Misti rolled her eyes and huffed over to the auditorium doors and almost dislocated her arm trying to jerk the door open.

"Geez, and you didn't even tell me it was locked? You're really weird, Laurie."

She turned and huffed away in the direction of the lockers.

Laurie suppressed a snicker. She'd better get it together. She really didn't want a reputation as the school crazy.

"So you think that's an option?" Bud was doing that scary-eyes thing again. It freaked Laurie out.

"What's an option?"

"Breaking in? Because I think I could do it. I've read about it, in books."

"No!" Laurie looked around to see if anyone had

heard. "Sheesh, Bud, are you insane? We'll come back tomorrow morning. It's got to be in there. We'll find it for sure."

"Yeah, you're right." Bud said. He didn't really want to start a life of crime anyway, even if he thought he probably could.

"Laurie?" A voiced echoed down the empty hallway. Misti was hurrying toward them waving a silver sweater over her head.

"I found it! Can you believe it? I left it in Mrs. Hutchins's room. I barely got it before she left for the day." Misti grinned at them. "Hey, do you need a ride? I called my mom to come get me in case I missed the late bus."

"Yeah, great!" Bud yelled quickly. He hadn't even thought about what to do if the late bus left, and that was just the kind of lack of planning that made his dad crazy. Bud leaned over to Laurie. "Want to meet early tomorrow? We'll research tonight and find it in the morning. This'll be a piece of cake. And besides, we've got plenty of time."

Laurie didn't even have time to argue before Bud had grabbed his backpack and started for Misti. It wasn't like they had a lot of choices, though.

"Thanks, Misti, you're the best!" Bud yelled, doing his plodding run up the hallway.

Laurie trudged silently after him.

Misti frowned. "Oh. Okay. Yeah." She shot Laurie an evil glare. "Bud's coming too. Greeeat."

Note from Horace Wallace Jr. to Horace Wallace Sr.

Hi Dad,
I need to work on a school project before class tomorrow, so I'm going to take the early bus in the morning. I left my spelling and math drills on the table, and I made burritos. Yours is in the fridge.
Bud

Note from Horace Wallace Sr. to Horace Wallace Jr.

Good job on the drills, Son.

Bud and Laurie sat in front of the auditorium watching the buses roll in. They'd done a search, but unless the treasure was hidden under the stage somewhere or in the catwalks (which seemed perfect to Laurie, but too dangerous for Maria Tutweiler to consider to Bud), it wasn't in the auditorium.

"Do you think we missed it somehow?" Bud said.

Laurie shook her head. "If it was in there, we would've spotted it. And it's not Mrs. Reynolds, remember? It's the cat. And there was nothing about cats in there. Except the catwalk," she added under her breath.

"She wouldn't have wanted kids climbing fifty feet in the air, Laurie," Bud said for what felt like the fiftieth time.

"Fine," Laurie said. "So we're back to the cat, which doesn't seem to exist. We just need to find out if she really had one." She did a mental scan of all the people she'd seen in the school so far. "We need to talk to someone. Someone old. Real old."

"You think there's someone here old enough to remember whether Mrs. Reynolds had a cat? That's a stretch, don't you think?" Bud rubbed his nose, making it look like a snout again. Laurie tried to ignore it.

"Well, it's worth a shot, right? Who's the oldest person here? Mr. Murphy?"

Mr. Murphy was the band director. Word around school was that he liked to take his teeth out while he was leading the band. Bud shook his head. "I think he just looks old. We need somebody ancient."

Bud snapped his fingers just as Laurie's eyes brightened. They smirked at each other. "Miss Lucille."

**Miss Lucille's Daily Old Person Checklist
as imagined by Laurie Madison, grade six**

1. Ancient furry cardigan—check.
2. Puffy salon hairdo—check.
3. Orthopedic nurse-type shoes—check.
4. Papery-dry hands—check.
5. Oversized clip-on earrings—check.
6. Dusting of Eau d'Old Age—check.

Bud and Laurie raced into the library, slamming into the front desk and gasping for air. Miss Lucille, in the process of stamping a book, clutched her chest like she was having palpitations.

"Miss Lucille! Hi! We want to ask you . . ." Laurie gasped, trying to look composed and together. Miss Lucille stared at her like she'd never seen her before in her life. Which she hadn't, as a student, but she'd met Laurie plenty of times at Clucker reunions, so it's not like Laurie was an alien creature.

"It's about the school. Questions. About the school."

Bud apparently was in even worse shape than Laurie. He was not used to all that running.

"About Mrs. Reynolds? We want to ask . . . Mrs. Reynolds?" Laurie looked pleadingly at Miss Lucille.

Miss Lucille stopped clutching her chest, and the lightbulb seemed to go off over her head. Then her eyes teared up and she hurried over to Laurie, putting her arm around her and leading her gently to one of the reading tables.

"Oh, you poor dear," she clucked. "You poor, poor dear."

She sat Laurie down at the table and stared at her, patting her hand consolingly. "I'm so sorry to tell you this dear. But Mrs. Reynolds? I don't quite know how to say this. She's passed on."

Laurie tried her best to keep her face blank and neutral and not shoot Bud the "holy cow" look that she was dying to give. Because, holy cow.

Laurie nodded sadly. "Yes. I heard. It's very sad."

Miss Lucille stopped patting long enough to fish a handkerchief out of her sleeve and dab her eyes. "Oh, yes, it is. Lovely woman, she was. So sweet to me when I was your age. Don't make them like Lucinda Reynolds anymore. That's the truth."

Laurie nodded solemnly. She didn't know how she was going to bring up a cat now. It felt sacrilegious almost.

Bud didn't seem to have any problems, though. He sidled up to the table, nodded sadly, and then sat down.

"So did she have a cat?"

"What?" Miss Lucille looked shocked.

"We heard she had a cat."

Real slick, Bud. Laurie couldn't help but roll her eyes.

"We were hoping you could tell us about her cat." Laurie gave Miss Lucille a significant look.

Miss Lucille stopped dabbing for a moment and then teared up even worse. Dropping the handkerchief, she grabbed Laurie's hand.

"Oh, you poor dear." She said. "Oh, you poor, poor dear. I don't know how to say this."

"Passed on?" Bud cut in. He wasn't going to go through the whole routine again.

"Yes, it was very sad. That Homer was quite a cat. Don't make them like her anymore, no they don't."

"Homer?" Laurie's ears pricked up. "His name was Homer?"

"That's right." Miss Laurie leaned in and whispered conspiratorially. "But Homer was a she. Can you imagine? A boy's name for a girl cat." Miss Lucille went at it with the handkerchief again. Laurie got the idea she hadn't enjoyed herself so much in years. "Beautiful little calico. Used to roam the halls. Lucinda Reynolds was the head of the English department, you know, so she named her after the poet."

"When did Homer die? Is she buried anywhere around here?" Bud leaned forward, ignoring the daggers that Laurie was shooting at him. "Just checking all the angles, okay?" he muttered under his breath.

"We want to pay our respects," Laurie explained. The last thing they needed was for Miss Lucille to think they were pervy grave robbers or something.

"Oh, I don't know, dear. She was a cat, you know. I'm not sure what happened to her."

"Oh." Laurie was itching to get away, but Miss Lucille had her hand in a vise grip. She had some muscles for an old lady.

Laurie gave Bud what she hoped was a significant look. He nodded his head slightly. He'd had a lightbulb moment too. That clue was all about Mrs. Reynolds's real life actual cat. And if it roamed the halls, everybody would've known it.

"Those were the days." Miss Lucille sighed, waving her handkerchief like she was the belle of the ball. "They were so proud of that cat. And that bust they had made. Didn't look a thing like her, but Maria and Lucinda used to laugh and laugh over it."

"Bust?" Laurie held her breath. "Of a cat? Did they move it? I haven't seen it anywhere."

"Oh, yes, the bust of Homer. I'm sure you've seen it, hon, it's right where it always has been. Not a good likeness at all. Doesn't look anything like a cat."

"The English hall. The bust of Homer in the English hall," Bud breathed. Miss Lucille nodded and sighed. They weren't going to get more confirmation than that.

Laurie jumped to her feet, hand still attached to Miss Lucille. "Thanks, Miss Lucille! We'll, uh, pay our respects to the statue? Will that be okay? Right now, if you don't mind."

"What she said," Bud said, backing toward the door.

Miss Lucille looked confused, but she let go of Laurie's hand. "Whatever you say, dear. If you think that's best."

"Oh, it's the best, all right," Laurie said. "It's the best!"

PART THREE

HOMER'S SECRET

HOMER

"Is he really gone?" Laurie's leg was almost asleep by the time the bearded English teacher had locked his classroom and gone off whistling down the hall. But there was no way she was risking being spotted by that Keats fanatic again.

"Finally." Bud sighed. He was going to be in so much trouble if he got another tardy. But he wasn't about to leave now and miss the next clue.

Laurie and Bud waited another few minutes to be sure Mr. Beardy wasn't just faking them out and then hurried down to the bust of Homer.

It was sitting in its nook just as it had earlier, so it didn't look like anyone else had come poking around. Not that anyone would, but Laurie was still relieved.

Laurie and Bud looked at it reverently for a few moments, and then, at the same time, they attacked. Laurie threw her arms around Homer's head and tried hauling him out of the nook while Bud started pushing and pulling every bit of Homer and the nook that stuck out—the nose, the ears, the chin, everything. But after a few minutes of mauling, two things became pretty obvious: Homer wasn't moving, and nothing would push in or pull out, which pretty much meant no secret compartments.

"Shoot," Laurie said, staring at the poet gloomily. He stared back with his weird pupilless eyes. Laurie shivered. Those eyes gave her the creeps. And the hairdo wasn't helping much either. He had long curly side hair and a long curly beard, which may have been fashionable in Homer's time but wasn't doing him any favors these days. And around the base of the bust was a whole string of musical notes. There was some kind of arty diagonal design behind him in the nook, but nothing was jumping out at Laurie screaming, "Clue! Over here! I'm a clue!"

"Well, that was lame," Laurie said. "Maybe we're wrong?"

Bud shook his head. "No, I think this is it. We just aren't seeing it yet."

Laurie and Bud dedicated a long moment to seeing it.

"Yeah, still not seeing it," Laurie said finally.

"Me either." Bud groaned as the bell rang.

EMAIL
FROM: WALKER LEFRANCO, School Board President
TO: PRINCIPAL MARTIN WINKLE, Tuckernuck Hall
SUBJECT: GIVE IT UP, WINKLE

WINKLE:

We both know the school is going to close at the end of the fall semester. We both know your appeals don't hold water. That's a given. This is what I want to find out: is there any way to speed this up? Why wait until the end of the semester? Seems to me that we should just tear the Band-Aid off quickly.

— LEFRANCO

EMAIL

FROM: PRINCIPAL MARTIN WINKLE, Tuckernuck Hall
TO: WALKER LEFRANCO, School Board President
RE: GIVE IT UP, WINKLE

Thanks for your message. Let's just let the review process work the way it's intended, why don't we?
Best,
Martin

Laurie put on her Cluckers hat and held her notebook up close to her face. Sure, she was probably being a little overly cautious. Paranoid, even. But she wasn't going to let that bearded English freak spot her, and she wasn't going to miss her chance at solving the clue either. Bud was already staring at Homer when she got there.

"I can't believe this is supposed to be the cat," he said without looking up. "That's really not very fair."

"I know." Laurie glared at Homer. Mrs. Tutweiler thought she was so cute, with her lame clues and everything. Maybe they were easy and clever eighty years ago, but they sure weren't funny now.

"Anything?" she said, keeping one eye out for the English teacher.

"Nothing." Bud sighed.

"Maybe it'll come to us over the weekend. In a big flash of inspiration."

"It sure better." Bud tugged on one of the legs dangling from Laurie's hat and headed off to the bus.

GOALS FOR HORACE WALLACE JR.
compiled by Horace Wallace Sr.
1. Memorize the periodic chart, quiz on
   Saturday.
2. Memorize countries of Africa, quiz on
   Sunday.

3. Work on panorama of battlefield
   strategies of the Revolutionary War,
   battle this Saturday at 0900 hours!
4. Continue spelling study, dictionary letter
   Ea–Ec.
5. Word problems, chapter six.
6. Conjugate Latin verbs, workbook pages
   45-55.

ACTUAL GOALS FOR BUD WALLACE
compiled by Bud Wallace

1. Find dictionary big enough to hide book on
   Homer.
2. Figure out where next clue is.
3. Figure out convincing reason for staying after
   school.
4. Figure out way to "accidentally" destroy
   panorama. Or even better, for Dad to
   destroy it, so it's not my fault.

ALSO

5. Possibly convince school board to bring
   sweets back?
6. If number five not possible, win over
   classmates with terrific personality.

＝

Laurie threw her books down on her bed and then headed back out to Kimmy's house. She'd barely talked to Kimmy since school started. She'd known going to different schools would mean they'd hang out less, until she could transfer at least, but she hadn't expected it to be so much less.

She couldn't wait to fill Kimmy in about the treasure.

Sure, technically, she wasn't supposed to say anything to anybody, but it's not like Kimmy was going to blab. She wasn't even a Clucker, so who would she possibly say something to? She'd be like one of those consultants or something. Bud wouldn't care.

Laurie had almost managed to convince herself of that when she knocked on Kimmy's front door.

The sound of laughter hit her as Mrs. Baranski opened the door. "Laurie!" she said happily, giving Laurie a hug. "We've missed you! Come on in." She ushered Laurie into the entryway. "Kimmy will be so glad to see you. She's got a few of her new friends from Hamilton over."

"Oh. Um." Laurie froze. It never occurred to her that Kimmy might have people over.

Kimmy came shooting down the stairs with two

giggly girls behind her. "Laurie! I can't believe it!" She
turned to the girls on the stairs. "Steffie, Kendra, this is
Laurie, that girl from my old school. Laurie, come on
up, we were just about to play that karaoke game I got."

Laurie tried to smile, but her stomach felt all twisted.
The last thing she wanted to do was sing in front of
these two girls she didn't know. Especially since she was
apparently just that girl from Kimmy's old school.

"Thanks, but I don't . . ." Laurie hesitated. She'd been
dying to see Kimmy all week. But there was no way she
could tell her about the treasure now.

"What? It's karaoke time, Laurie!" Kimmy shifted
impatiently. "Are you in or out?"

Laurie took a deep breath. "I can't really. I just
wanted to come say hi. I've got a thing. At the library.
You know."

"Oh, sure, okay," Kimmy said. "Well, come back
soon, okay?"

"Yeah, oka—"

"Bye! Call me!" Kimmy was racing back up the stairs
with Steffi and Kendra before Laurie had even finished
her sentence.

Mrs. Baranski patted her awkwardly on the shoulder
and held the door open for her. "Come back soon, hon,

okay? She's just making new friends."

"Yeah." Laurie headed out onto the stoop. "Sure I will."

—✍—

"So basically, we both found out the exact same things about Homer," Laurie said on Monday. She'd headed to the library after the fiasco at Kimmy's house, because the last thing she wanted to do was have to explain why she was back so soon. Sure, it would've been tangible proof how Tuckernuck was ruining her life, but she just wasn't ready to look like that much of a loser yet, even to her mom.

At least Bud seemed happy to see her. They'd waited until the coast was clear in the English hall and then hurried over to the bust of Homer. "Ancient Greek poet, *Odyssey*, *Iliad*, blah blah blah. Big bunch of nothing."

She glared at the creepy eyes of the bust. "We're missing something big here."

Bud looked at his notes. "I don't know what it could be. Maybe you're right and we're wrong about this whole thing? Maybe there's something else called Homer. Maybe the cat's grave or something?"

Laurie shook her head. "That can't be it. Miss Lucille said they acted all weird about the bust, remember?

This has to be right."

"Yeah, but I thought there'd be another note and letter. You know, like last time." Bud kicked at some kid's lost multiple-choice test on the floor.

"Yeah, me too." Laurie ran a finger along the edge of Homer's head. "But I guess she couldn't do that every time. It's too obvious."

"I guess." Bud stared at the bust of Homer again and the elaborate decorated base. He frowned. "Weird. That doesn't make sense. Hey, Laurie . . ."

He glanced over at her, but Laurie didn't seem to be paying attention to him. She was squinching up her face and doing the thousand-mile stare at Homer. Bud decided he'd work it out in his head before he called her back from dreamland or wherever she was.

"Hey, Bud, does that look like a big A to you?" she said finally.

"What? Where?" Bud said distractedly. He'd really felt like he was on to something, and Laurie was messing up his train of thought.

"Right there." Laurie pointed at the diagonal lines behind the bust. "It looks like a big A, right behind him. Don't you think?"

Bud looked at the lines behind the bust of Homer

and felt like smacking himself on the head. He couldn't believe he hadn't noticed it right away. It was definitely a huge A carved into the nook behind Homer.

"But that doesn't make any sense. Why would you put a big A behind him? Because he's Greek? And he's the alpha or something?" That didn't really sound right to Bud, though. "It must be there for a reason."

"Wait, do you think . . ." Laurie dug around in her pocket and pulled out the wooden D from the Hilda frame. She held it up in front of Homer and smirked. "See—it's the same type of letter." Laurie turned to Bud happily. "It matches! It's part of the clue!"

Bud nodded. The D and the A were both the same stylized kind of letter. It was all coming together. "I think you're right. Why else would there be a big A there?" Bud took a step back to take in the whole scene: the bust, the nook, the base, everything. And then it all clicked.

He tried to fight the excitement rising in his chest. He didn't want to come off like a big arm-waving freak in case his theory sounded stupid out loud.

"And look at this here." He pointed to the music at the base of the statue.

"This music down here?" he said, carefully controlling

his voice so he didn't start laughing maniacally. "What does Homer have to do with music? Nothing, right?"

"Right." Laurie nodded. At least, the encyclopedia at the library hadn't mentioned anything.

Bud gave her a significant look. "Sooo?"

Laurie gasped. "Oh, my gosh. So you think . . ."

Bud nodded. "I think it's a clue! It doesn't fit with Homer, right? So if it doesn't fit with him, it must fit with the next clue!"

"You're right! You're right! That must be it!" Laurie squealed, jumping up and down. Laurie didn't mind being an arm-waving freak. Bud was right—that music didn't make any sense otherwise. And if it turned out they were wrong, the music wouldn't lead them any-where and they'd figure it out soon enough. "Maybe it's another title clue. Or do you think the notes spell some-thing? Can you read music?"

Bud made a face. "Not really. Sort of. A little. But we should copy this down. That way we don't have to stand around here forever, attracting attention."

Laurie looked puzzled. "What do you mean?"

Bud jerked his head the side. The bearded Keats enthusiast—who, a little research had revealed, was called Mr. Sanchez—was standing in the doorway of his classroom, smiling over at them.

"Oh, crud," Laurie said. She pulled out a notebook and fumbled for a pencil. "This is going to take forever too, making the little lines for the notes and all? He's going to come over here, isn't he?"

Bud shook his head. "Forget that. It'll be easier on sheet music paper. I know where they have some. I'll make a copy."

Laurie nodded gratefully, held her notebook up to shield her face, and raced down the hallway like she was a celebrity avoiding paparazzi. Mr. Sanchez was totally fooled. At least he didn't come chasing after Laurie, so same difference, as far as she was concerned.

Bud reached out and touched the notes on the base of the bust. He hadn't felt this good in a long time. Smiling to himself, he hurried after her.

**Ways to Elude a Persistent and Overeager English Teacher
by Laurie Madison, grade six**

1. NEVER make eye contact.
2. Feign illness (vomiting on cue—always a winner).
3. Make excuses and back away slowly.

4. Agree to anything and never return to the scene.
5. Run for your life.
6. Feign death (only in extreme circumstances).

Boneheaded Statement of the Day
by Bud Wallace
"Music paper? No problem! I know where to get that."

Bud stood at the end of the music hall, biting his lip. He didn't know why he'd said he knew where to find music paper. Sure, it was true, but the last place he wanted to go was the music hall.

The teacher he'd seen earlier was standing outside her classroom talking to another teacher. She wasn't acting like she'd spotted him, but Bud knew she knew he was there. She was just waiting for him, he could tell.

Pete Simkins slammed into Bud from behind and pushed past him without a word. Bud sighed. Forget the music paper. It wasn't worth the risk, and standing around was just making things worse. Besides, drawing his own wasn't that big a deal.

Bud turned to go and promptly slammed into Calliope Judkin.

"Oh, hey, Bud. I didn't know you took music." Calliope smiled.

Bud raised his eyebrows. He hadn't expected Calliope to stop and talk to him, let alone smile. He'd pretty much stopped expecting people to talk to him last year, when it became obvious that even the black-market Skittles supply had been cut off for good.

"Yeah, I don't," Bud said. Suddenly he was struck with inspiration. "Do you?"

Calliope nodded and smiled again. She didn't even seem ready to rush off or anything. Bud took that as a sign. "Could you snag me a piece of music paper? A blank piece. I just . . . I don't want to go down there right now. That teacher wants me to do chorus."

Calliope looked over Bud's shoulder and nodded knowingly. "Miss Downey. Makes sense. Hold on one sec."

Calliope turned, trotted down the hallway, and disappeared into a classroom. In a second she was back, holding out a piece of music paper.

"Thanks, Calliope. You're the best." Bud reached for the paper, but just as his hand closed around it, Calliope snatched it out of Bud's reach.

"Not so fast, Bud. What's this for?" Calliope smiled again, but it didn't seem like such a friendly smile anymore. "Just curious."

Bud hesitated. It's not like he could tell her. Calliope's name had been specifically mentioned in the don't-tell-anyone instructions. Laurie would kill him. And besides, Calliope seemed a little more than "just curious." More like cats are "just curious" about what mice are up to. But he had to say something. "I . . . it's nothing. Just . . ."

"Does it have something to do with Laurie Madison?"

Bud sucked in his breath and cursed his lousy poker face as Calliope smirked triumphantly. He knew he'd probably just given away the whole game. But it's not like he would just spill the beans now.

"No. It's, uh . . ." He searched wildly for a plausible explanation. "It's the auditions. I'm working on something. I really am auditioning, see. I was just pretending before."

Calliope's eyes narrowed. "I didn't see your name on the sign-up list."

Bud attempted a nonchalant laugh but ended up making a weird squeaking sound instead. "Yeah, I'm shy, okay? And I'm still working on my piece. That's why I need the paper—to work things out. Thanks, bye!" He snatched the paper out of Calliope's hand and dashed off down the hallway.

Once he'd rounded the corner, Bud tucked the paper into his notebook and smiled. He was pretty slick, if he did say so himself. Calliope didn't suspect a thing.

Suspicious Activities/Mysteries to
Investigate
by Calliope Judkin
1. Tutweiler Treasure: Determine location
   ASAP. Collect accolades, glory, etc.
2. Cafeteria mystery meat: What could it
   possibly be? Question cafeteria lady, aka
   Bonnie the Net.
3. Bud Wallace and Laurie Madison: what
   are they hiding? Possible story there?
   CONTINUE TAIL.

Question of the Day
by Laurie Madison, grade six
What would Bud and Calliope Judkin have to talk about? Besides plotting to find the treasure and cut me out completely, that is. Just wondering.

Bud fell into a chair next to Laurie in the cafeteria. "Success!" he said, slapping the music paper onto the table and smirking at Laurie and Misti.

"So how's Calliope?" Laurie said, folding her arms. "You two have a nice talk?"

"Huh?" Bud felt like he'd wandered into the wrong conversation. Or a minefield. Both seemed likely.

Misti Pinkerton dropped her tuna sandwich back onto the plastic wrap. "What, is this an everyday thing? Every day, Laurie?"

"Not every day, okay?" Laurie grumbled. "We're working on a thing."

"Oh, okay. If it's a *thing*," Misti groused, picking up her sandwich and finishing it off in one bite. "I've lost my appetite."

Bud watched as Misti crumpled up her empty lunch

bag. "Yeah, I can tell," he said, grinning at Laurie.

Misti glared at him and stalked off without a backward glance.

"Way to go, Bud." Laurie snickered. "So you got it?"

Bud pushed the piece of paper over to her. "I told you getting the paper would be no problem. I copied it exactly, so we don't have to worry about Sanchez every second."

"That's great," Laurie said. Every time she went down that hallway, she knew she was pressing her luck. It was getting to the point where she felt like she needed a disguise just to go to Mr. Robinson's class.

She looked at the piece of paper in front of her. Bud had done a good job copying the notes down, but it still didn't make any sense to her. "Do you know what it is?"

Bud shook his head. "I'm not sure. I'm kind of sketchy on the whole reading-music thing."

"Maybe it spells something? I took piano once—how does it go? All Good Birds Do Fly?"

Bud nodded. "Close. Every Good Bird Does Fly. That's the lines. And the spaces are FACE. So that makes this . . ."

He screwed up his face in concentration. "That makes this . . . C-E-D-G-C-D-E-C-E-C-D-G . . ."

"G-D-E-C," Laurie finished. "So much for spelling something. Sheesh, is there even one word in that mess?"

"Well, it was a good idea anyway." Bud sighed. "I don't know how we're going to figure this one out. Google's not going to help if it's another title clue."

Laurie made a face. "Tell me about it." She pushed the paper away. "We need to hear it, that's what we need. And I don't think I can pick this out on the piano. If we even had a piano."

Bud pulled the paper a little closer, and his ears turned bright red. "I might . . . see, my mom . . . I took piano once too. I could give it a try."

Laurie leaned back in her chair and gave him a long, hard stare. "It would mean going to the music hall. Unless you've got a portable keyboard in your backpack."

Bud shrugged. "It's no problem. We'll head to the music hall after gerbil time. No big deal."

Laurie raised her eyebrows. The music hall was as bad for Bud as the English hall was for her.

Bud squirmed under her stare. "What? Seriously, I think all the spots for chorus auditions are full anyway. I couldn't audition if I wanted to. No sweat."

**Sixth-Grade Chorus
Audition Sign-Up Sheet**

1. Trinity Harbaugh
2. Sam Silver
3. Misti Pinkerton
4. Pete Simkins
5. Sheila Weston
6. Calliope Judkin
7. Hannah Stoller
8.
9.
10.
11.
12.
13.

Laurie had just finished feeding Ponch and Jon when she saw Misti go by in her Clucker hat. Laurie almost dropped the bag of sunflower seeds. The last thing she needed right now was another Clucker function.

"Misti, wait up!" Laurie hurried out of the classroom and fell into step next to Misti. She tried not to look at the hat. It was hard to keep a straight face with a doofy stuffed chicken watching you, but this was serious. "So, what's up?"

"Not much. Just, you know. Going to my locker." Misti looked confused. "Why?"

Laurie cleared her throat. Better just come out with it. "What's with the hat?"

Misti grinned. "Cool, isn't it? I figured, I'm a Clucker, right? And there's nothing that says I can only wear the hat at official Clucker functions." She twirled a dangly chicken leg. "Besides, it's cute, right?"

Laurie bit her lip hard. At least somebody was having fun being a Clucker. "Right. Really cute. It's a good look for you."

Misti shrugged. "Thanks! Cluck cluck cluck, Laurie!" she crowed.

Laurie's eyes got wide as she watched Misti bounce off down the hallway. "The fight song!"

She raced back inside and grabbed Bud by the arm.

"Hey! Bruising, remember?" Bud scowled.

"Yeah, sorry about that." Laurie let go of Bud's arm like it was a hot potato. "But Misti! And the hat! And the fight song! Right?"

Bud folded his arms and waited. He figured that Laurie would start making sense eventually. His patience paid off.

"I bet that music—it's the fight song, right?"

Bud smacked his thigh with his hand, scaring the crap out of Ponch and Jon. (Literally, unfortunately.) "That's got to be it! Let's get to that piano. We'll be able to recognize that song, no problem."

Bud grabbed his backpack and pulled the folded sheet of music out of his pocket. After making sure there was no chance of a Ponch and Jon jailbreak during the night, he and Laurie bounded off down the hallway into the Music hall. There was a piano in the first classroom—they'd seen it the other day. They were just a couple of awkward one-fingered notes away from solving the clue.

They were running so fast that they were hardly paying attention to anything around them, so they'd already hurried into the room before the truth dawned on them. Someone was playing the piano.

Miss Downey looked up and smiled as they skittered to a halt. "I had a feeling you'd turn up— Bud, is it? Take your place along the wall. You'll be coming up soon." She motioned to the left side of the classroom, where students were lined up waiting their turn.

It was the choral auditions.

Bud turned whiter than his shirt collar and looked

helplessly at Laurie. "But I . . ."

"Don't be shy, Bud. Don't think I haven't seen you hanging around. I could tell you wanted to audition. I'm just glad you decided to join us." Miss Downey turned to Laurie. "Are you auditioning too?"

Bud still stood gaping at her, his face stricken. A little bead of sweat had formed and started to trickle down his temple. Laurie gave him an apologetic grin and then turned back to Miss Downey.

"Nope, can't sing a note, unfortunately. I'm just here for moral support." She smacked Bud on the arm. "Break a leg, Bud. I know you'll be great. See you!"

Then she turned and raced out.

Bud gave her one last desperate look as she disappeared out the door. Then he felt Miss Downey's hands clamp on to his shoulders and pull him farther inside the room.

**PROOF THAT BUD WALLACE IS A BIG BOY
AND CAN TAKE CARE OF HIMSELF
also known as
Why It Was Okay to Ditch Him
by Laurie Madison, grade six**
1. It's singing. Nobody died from singing, right?

2. Possibility of amusement later on: high.
3. Had to save self. Sad fact of life.

"So?" Laurie was sitting on the steps waiting for the late bus when Bud walked out of the school. She'd been feeling occasional twinges of guilt for ditching him, and seeing him stagger out like a zombie cinched it for her. It was official. She was a bad person, all right.

Bud slumped down next to her. "Second tenor. Rehearsals twice a week."

Laurie stared at him in horror and then burst out laughing. "I'm so sorry!" she gasped, tears running down her face. "It's just so . . . man, that's awful! Second tenor? For real?"

Bud just nodded. "She said I had a voice like an angel."

Laurie managed to keep a straight face for a whole minute before she lost it again. Bud lasted two.

⸺

Laurie waited until Mrs. Madison was busy making dinner to sneak downstairs and fire up the old Casio keyboard taking up space in the rec room. Bud had torn off the bottom part of the music paper and copied the notes onto it for her while they waited for the late bus. After a quick check to make sure Jack wasn't lurking around anywhere with a smart remark at the ready, she propped the (now grubby-looking) piece of paper in front of the keyboard and softly tried to pick out the notes. But it was no use. It wasn't coming back to her like she'd hoped it would. She'd only gotten through three of them when Mr. Madison stuck his head into the room. And she wasn't even sure those three were right.

Laurie cursed silently to herself. She hadn't realized her dad was home yet. He was even worse than her mom.

"What's up, Laurie?" he said hopefully.

She quickly snatched her fingers away from the keyboard. "Nothing much." She tried not to look at the paper propped up on the table. Mr. Madison didn't seem to have noticed it.

"Should I call Mrs. Rosenbaum? I know she'd love to have you back." He gave a tentative smile. Mr. Madison brought out the keyboard an average of once a year in the hopes of luring Laurie back into piano lessons. So far it hadn't worked. It would've had a better chance if he'd stopped playing the Mrs. Rosenbaum card.

Mrs. Rosenbaum was Laurie's piano teacher from first grade. She lived down the street with six cats, more afghan throws and doilies than any one person should ever have, and a ruler, which she liked to use to whack people on the knuckles when they got their fingering wrong. Laurie flexed her fingers at the memory. She'd gotten her fingering wrong a lot.

"That's okay. I was just messing around. No big deal."

Mr. Madison came farther into the room and put his hands in his pockets. "Anything in particular?"

"Just . . ." Laurie leaned back, carefully crumpling the piece of paper in her fist behind her back. "I just was trying to remember how the fight song went. Just the main part."

"Aha! Tuckernuck Cluckers." Mr. Madison grinned. "I could tell you were getting more settled at that school. Let's see if I remember."

He bent over the keyboard and, with a flourish, played the Tuckernuck Cluckers fight song from beginning to end. Complete with singing and heartfelt clucking.

Laurie clucked along, but her heart wasn't in it. She didn't know what song was on that piece of paper, but it definitely wasn't what her dad was playing.

Bud threw his books on the table in the entryway and snuck into the formal living room, cringing at the noise his feet made on the plastic rug protectors. His mother's old piano was there, but Bud hadn't heard anyone play it in ages. He hoped it was still in tune. He was just sitting down at the piano bench when his dad came through the front door.

Bud jumped guiltily to his feet. He wished he'd thought to bring one of his schoolbooks along as a decoy, just in case.

Mr. Wallace stopped and looked at Bud for a long minute before putting his briefcase on the floor next to the table. "Playing the piano?"

"No, just dusting. Tidying up." Bud cringed inwardly at how dumb that sounded. "I'm sorry."

Mr. Wallace nodded. "That's your mother's piano." He rubbed the edge of it lightly. "No one plays it anymore."

"I was just taking a break. I wasn't playing it," Bud said, pushing the bench back in. "Gotta hit the books, right?"

Mr. Wallace nodded slowly and patted Bud on the back as he hurried upstairs.

Bud made a new entry on his list of goals when he got upstairs. Figuring out that song had a new place at number one.

EMAIL

FROM: PRINCIPAL MARTIN WINKLE, Tuckernuck Hall

TO: SAVE TUCKERNUCK ALUMNI ORGANIZATION

SUBJECT: SAVE TUCKERNUCK RALLY

I wanted to let you all know how much I appreciate the Save Tuckernuck Hall rally scheduled later this week. I'm afraid the school board president is going to take some convincing before he agrees to keep Tuckernuck open, and I'm hoping this rally will do the trick. Keep clucking!

Marty

Bud raced from the bus to the music room in the morning. He figured he'd take five minutes, figure out the song, and look pretty impressive when he had all the answers at lunch.

Too bad the music room was locked when he got there. And too bad Laurie had had the same idea. She was sitting in front of the door doing her math homework when Bud showed up.

"No dice," she said, hardly looking up. "It's locked. And I don't even know if Miss Downey has a first period."

Bud groaned. "We've got to figure it out!"

"Well, it's not the fight song, I can tell you that much."

Bud couldn't believe it. How the heck did she know? "What? Are you sure?"

Laurie nodded. "My dad played it last night. It's not the same at all. Not enough notes."

Bud sat down next to her. "Shoot. Well, we can figure it out anyway. I think I can figure out how it goes. We'll do it as soon as they unlock the door."

"Hi, guys. Miss Downey doesn't have a homeroom. What are you doing?"

Bud and Laurie looked up to see Calliope Judkin coming toward them. She was smiling, but her eyes were narrow and suspicious.

"Or we'll do it at lunch," Bud muttered, standing up. "Just leaving is what I was doing, Calliope. See you." He stalked off down the hallway. He didn't know what Calliope's issue was, following him around like that. There was only one explanation, as far as he could see. She must like him. He shook his head. Poor kid. Hard to blame her.

Laurie ignored Calliope's stare and continued working on her math homework. Or at least she pretended to, by writing down random numbers. It was impossible to concentrate with Calliope's eyes boring into her skull like that. She just hoped Mr. Mercado didn't collect the homework today.

"You two sure are spending a lot of time together these days," Calliope said. "You and Bud Wallace. Nice of you to be friends with the class outcast." She was trying to act casual and conversational, but Laurie knew better.

"We're working on a project, Calliope. We're not friends. It's a thing," Laurie said into her textbook. Unfortunately, that explanation didn't work as well on Calliope as it did on Misti.

"A thing? What kind of thing? For what class?"

"We're both Gerbil Monitors, okay?" Laurie said, slamming her book shut and standing up. "It's gerbil business. You wouldn't understand." She shoved her book into her backpack and headed off down the hallway, hoping Calliope wouldn't think too hard about what she'd just said. Because gerbil business totally didn't make sense. It wasn't like Ponch and Jon were starting a band and needed managers or something. Laurie wished she was better with the snappy comebacks.

Thankfully, Calliope didn't say anything. She just took out a small notebook and made a careful notation inside.

Possible Gerbil Monitor Projects
by Calliope Judkin

1. Gerbil care? No reason for out-of-classroom association.
2. Gerbil relocation project? Gerbils not moving, no reason.
3. Gerbil study activities? But they're not studying anything, and neither are the gerbils.
4. Gerbil safety issues? Gerbils inside glass aquariums are pretty safe.

CONCLUSION:
They're lying. No possible gerbil-related project.

Note from Calliope Judkin to Secret School Contact

I know you said you didn't want a paper trail leading back to you, but I think I've uncovered something suspicious. Laurie Madison and

Bud Wallace may be on to something. Possibly treasure related. I've seen them snooping around the school. I'm going to try to work my way into their confidence. I'll let you know more soon.
Calliope

Laurie and Bud chewed slowly, staring at the music in front of them. Laurie didn't even know why she was bothering to look, though—she could see the stupid notes when she closed her eyes. Even if she never found another clue, Laurie wanted to at least know what that music was before she died.

Bud squinshed up his eyes. "Maybe it's an anagram? Dec . . . Ged . . . no, that's sure not working."

Laurie sighed. "Code. Gotta be. Right?"

"Code? Okay. Code using what? What kind of code?"

"Beats me. Geez, why can't she give us an easy one, like 'look in the green box on the top shelf of the closet' or something." Laurie threw down her sandwich in disgust and picked up her backpack.

Bud shrugged. "We'll figure it out. Eventually."

Laurie snorted. Eventually was no good. She'd seen

the morning's paper. If they didn't solve the clue soon, they'd never solve it. They'd be picking the treasure out of the school rubble.

～

Laurie nodded to Miss Lucille as she headed into the library. Bud was hopeless, so it was up to her to crack this thing. She headed over to the music section and pulled out a random book of sheet music. *Great American Songs of the Early Twentieth Century*. Perfect. She'd figure out what song that was if she had to look at every song ever written.

Laurie slid into a seat at the table near the door and looked around. Just her luck—Calliope Judkin was two tables over, watching her with narrowed eyes. Laurie gave her a grim smile. If Calliope thought she'd get any clues from Laurie, she was sorely mistaken.

Someone had left an ancient brown book lying on the chair, so she propped it open and hid the songbook inside. Then she pulled the crumpled piece of music out of her pocket and started looking for a match.

She'd definitely ruled out "You're a Grand Old Flag," "On the Good Ship Lollipop," and "Elephant Rag" (which she had to admit she was curious about) when she felt the back of her neck prickle. Someone else was watching her. Laurie looked up casually and did a quick scan of the library. Mr. Sanchez was grinning at her from the stacks.

Great. Laurie gave him a half wave and tried to go back to her book, but he gave her a big thumbs-up and smiled again. What the heck? Laurie looked down in confusion and lost her grip on the sheet music book. It slid down, revealing the title of the ancient brown book. Laurie groaned. Keats.

Bud didn't think he could stand the sight of one more revolutionary soldier. He'd been working on his panorama for hours, and what he really wanted to do was go get the plastic dinosaurs that his mom had given him when he was little and launch a full-scale dinosaur attack, with lots of screaming and carnage. Those puny troops wouldn't last a minute against his T-Rex. But the dinosaurs were in a box in the attic somewhere, with the rest of the stuff his dad had packed away after his mom died. After they'd had their big talk where they decided to only focus on the important things. And no matter how you cut it, T-Rex battles didn't qualify as important.

Bud flicked one of the tiny soldiers into the Plasticine river and trudged up the basement stairs.

But when he got to the top of the stairs, he stopped short. If he didn't know better, he'd think someone was playing the piano. He could hear the notes hanging in the air. But he knew that couldn't be right.

He peeked around the corner into the formal living room. His dad was standing there, staring at the piano.

Bud cleared his throat. "Dad?"

Mr. Wallace jumped a little, but he didn't turn around.

"Were you playing the piano?"

Mr. Wallace turned around and smiled at Bud. "Of course not. Don't be silly."

"I just thought I heard . . ."

"A car just went by with the radio on. That must've been it. I'm sorry it upset you, Bud. It's gone now."

Bud nodded. But it hadn't sounded like a car radio.

The phone had rung six times. Laurie was about to hang up when Kimmy finally answered. "Kimmy?"

"Laurie! Hey, sorry I haven't called you back. I meant to, I really did, but you know . . . school's been crazy."

"Yeah, mine too! I really miss you!"

"Me too. Your parents are still letting you transfer, right?"

"I don't know yet." Laurie sat down on the bed.

"What? Why? Laurie, they've got to!" Kimmy wailed. "You'd love it at Hamilton, it's so cool, did I tell you about the cafeteria? Oh, my gosh, you aren't going to believe it. They have all these different stations, okay? And you can—"

"I'm working on it, Kimmy!" Laurie interrupted. She didn't really feel like hearing about how awesome things at Hamilton were. "Hey, you know that treasure story?"

"What? Treasure? That old story? Laurie, you've got to get out of there. Look, I've gotta go, I've got this pizza study thing with Kendra. I'd invite you, but it's for Hamilton people. But I'll call soon, okay?"

Laurie hung up with a weird feeling in the pit of her stomach. Ever since she'd been in school, it had been the same thing, Laurie and Kimmy, Kimmy and Laurie. The wonder twins, two peas in a pod, joined at the hip. They used to talk every night.

She'd been figuring that if she found the treasure, her parents would let her do whatever she wanted. But if she wasn't going to find it, she needed to figure out another way to get to Hamilton. And fast. Or else there wouldn't be any Laurie and Kimmy anymore. Just Laurie.

Bud and Laurie sat in the cafeteria staring gloomily at the piece of paper with the notes on it. Laurie sighed. This was it then. The end of the line. Maria Tutweiler had beaten them fair and square.

"We're going to have to accept it. She beat us."

"Oh, come on . . ."

"No, Bud. If it's words, we don't know them. If it's a title, we don't have it. The only thing we have left is playing the stupid song, which we can't do. Or asking for help, which we're not going to do. So we're beat."

"I'm not giving up, Laurie." Bud clenched his teeth.

"Fine, then figure it out." Laurie punched Bud on the shoulder. "Work those pipes, Chorus Boy. Can't you hum it? Because that's all we've got." Laurie tried to sound enthusiastic, but she failed miserably. Even if they managed to figure out what the song was, what good would it do? They wouldn't even know what to do with it.

Bud cleared his throat and looked around. His ears were getting red. "I could . . . okay. I guess." He cleared his throat again and attempted a rusty-sounding hum. Laurie gave him a sideways glance. Did Bud even use that voice? Didn't sound like an angel to her. She didn't say anything, though. She figured if she pointed out that he sounded like a creaky iron gate, he'd clam up altogether.

After a few more awkward throat clearings, Bud seemed to loosen up a little.

"Du du du du . . . hmmm." Bud hesitated. "Du du du du . . ." He glanced at Laurie to see if she was laughing at him, but she didn't seem to be. He relaxed a little and hummed a little louder. "Du du du du . . ."

"Du du du du." Misti joined in as she threw her lunch bag onto the table. "BOM BOM BOM. Three o'clock, time to go home! I wish."

Misti pulled out her sandwich, jerked her head at Bud, and rolled her eyes at Laurie. "Not every day, huh? Right."

Laurie and Bud stared at her openmouthed. Misti stopped midchew and looked nervously from one to the other. "What? It's the bell-tower clock chime, right? That's what you guys were doing?"

Bud and Laurie gasped and stared at each other. "The bell-tower clock chime!"

Misti let the sandwich drop onto the table. "You guys are freaking me out." She reached over and pulled the piece of paper toward her. "Is that it written out? What are you guys doing?"

Bud glanced at Laurie. "It's . . . uh."

"Sort of a scavenger hunt, that's all," Laurie said, not meeting Bud's eye. "No big deal."

"Ooh, I love scavenger hunts!" Misti's eyes brightened. "Is that your 'thing'? Can I help?"

"Well, sure, I guess—" Bud started, but Laurie kicked him under the table.

"We're not supposed to have any help," she said. "But maybe if we get really stuck?"

Misti looked disappointed. "I guess that makes sense. That's cool, though. What class is that for? I wish I had your teacher."

Bud looked panicked. "It's for . . . uh . . ."

"Hey, so chorus, huh?" Laurie cut him off. "You guys are going to be pretty busy, right?"

Misti perked back up. She immediately started in on an analysis of Miss Downey, of first tenor Sam Silver and his weird unidentifiable odors, and of the woeful pitch issues of Hannah Stoller. The scavenger hunt didn't come up again.

When the warning bell rang, Laurie elbowed Bud in the ribs. "It's in the bell tower. It's got to be," she whispered.

Bud nodded. "I know."

• PART FOUR •

STORMING THE TOWER

Laurie was doing the silent reading assignment in Mr. Robinson's class when she heard the door open. She probably wouldn't have even looked up if Bud hadn't done the audible gasping-so-hard-that-you-almost-choke-on-your-own-spit thing. And what she saw made her feel sick to her stomach.

Mr. Sanchez was standing at the front of the room, talking with Mr. Robinson. Which was bad, sure, but not bad enough to make Laurie want to feign a serious and fatal illness. But Mr. Sanchez was smiling and looking right at her while he talked. Laurie and Bud exchanged worried glances. This could not be good.

Laurie knew she needed to act fast. She did a quick mental inventory.

DEPLOYING THE GET-OUT-OF-CLASS SECRET WEAPON: Pros and Cons by Laurie Madison, grade six

SECRET WEAPON, also known as the ever-popular Vomiting on Cue.

PROS: Chance of success: very good.

CONS: New nickname—Pukey Girl.

"Good news, class," Mr. Robinson said, clapping his

hands together. He smiled that teacher smile that always means lots of extra work. Laurie eyed the door. It was too far away to make a run for it. "If you could give me your attention for a moment."

Mr. Robinson caught Laurie's eye and gave her an extra-big smile. Laurie stifled a groan. This was so not good.

"Mr. Sanchez here tells me that there's been particular interest this year in starting a Romantic English poets' club. That would be poets like Byron, Keats, Shelley. It sounds like an exciting idea, and we have our very own Laurie Madison to thank for it. Stand up, Laurie."

Standing up was the last thing in the world Laurie wanted to do. But apparently her legs weren't about to cross Mr. Robinson. Before she knew it, she was on her feet, swaying uncertainly. Mariah Jeffries in the second row shot her a nasty look. Mariah was not a poetry fan.

"Now if you're interested in joining this exciting club, the sign-up sheet is outside Mr. Sanchez's room, and as the club founder, Laurie can tell you all about it, so go to her with any questions or ideas. And in honor of the club, we'll be starting a new segment on the poets next week. Thank you, Laurie. Would you like to say anything about the club?" Mr. Robinson nodded at Laurie encouragingly.

"I'm going to be sick," Laurie muttered under her breath. Apparently her vocal cords were a little less obedient to Mr. Robinson.

"Speak up, Laurie," Mr. Robinson said.

Laurie's nerve failed her. She couldn't face going through the next few years as Pukey Girl Madison. "Keats is great," she said without enthusiasm. "Great club. Loads of fun."

She dropped back into her seat. Mariah was almost completely turned around in her seat, she was glaring at Laurie so hard.

Laurie put her head on her desk. But before she did, she couldn't help but notice Bud, staring straight ahead, his shoulders shaking with silent laughter.

~

"So, how does it feel to be club founder?" Bud smirked at Laurie as he filled Ponch and Jon's water bottle.

"Shut up, Bud." Laurie scowled, flinging gerbil food into the cage recklessly. Ponch and Jon scurried for the nearest toilet-paper tube to escape the unexpected sunflower seed flurries. "I am so not talking about it."

Bud chuckled under his breath. Chorus didn't seem so bad anymore.

Laurie ignored the chuckle. "Besides, the important thing is getting into that bell tower. Once we do, we can find the next clue and we'll have the whole night to think about it." She slammed the lid on Ponch and Jon's cage and grabbed her backpack. "Hurry up, okay? I'm not spending the weekend wondering what's in there."

Bud was learning when it was best not to argue with Laurie. He gave a salute of good-bye to the irritated rodents and hurried after Laurie toward the bell tower.

Sign on the bell-tower door

WARNING
DANGEROUS AREA
NO ACCESS
AUTHORIZED PERSONNEL ONLY

Laurie jerked the door handle in frustration for what seemed like the fiftieth time.

"I think it's still locked, Laurie," Bud said carefully. Laurie was going to rip her arm off if she wasn't careful. He'd never seen it happen before, but he was sure it was possible, especially the way she was pulling at that handle.

Laurie didn't answer. She just jerked the door again.

"We'll have to find another way in. I'm sure there's a key. We'll just get it somehow," Bud said, trying to talk her down. Laurie had a crazed look on her face that Bud was sure wasn't normal.

Laurie glared at Bud and jerked the door again. "Sure, and when's that going to be? Tomorrow? The next day? Next week? I can't take a whole weekend of waiting, Bud!"

Bud knew how she felt. But that wasn't going to magically open the door. Besides, the late bus was going to leave soon, and he hadn't even looked at his dictionary pages this week. His dad was going to be really disappointed in him.

Bud tried not to glance at his watch. "It'll give us time to plan and figure things out. We need to do that anyway, right? If it's locked, it's locked. Nothing we can do."

Laurie knew Bud was right. But that didn't mean she had to like it. Especially since it was coming from Mr. Hey-Let's-Break-Into-the-Auditorium. Nice time for him to turn all moral and law-abiding. She decided to give the door one last pull for good measure.

"Hey! You there—girlie, now, don't be tugging on that door. You're gonna hurt yourself." An angry voice interrupted Laurie midtug.

Laurie and Bud looked up to see a lanky, slick-haired janitor hurrying toward them with a scowl on his face. He was wearing a pair of coveralls with the name Reginald embroidered on the pocket. Laurie dropped the door handle and tried to put on her innocent face, but it was too late. Reginald had totally busted her.

"Now why are you messing with that door? Can't go in there, not a couple of kids like you. It's dangerous. Can't you read the sign?" Reginald shook his head at them, like he'd had high hopes for them and now those hopes were dashed.

Bud cleared his throat. "We just wanted to look at the bells. It's for class. A project." The project line got them every time.

But Reginald just pursed his lips in disgust. "Now don't give me that line, young man. There's not a teacher in this school who would assign you to go in there. It's too high, and not safe. Now get away from here. I've got my eye on you two. I'll know if you come around again."

Reginald pointed two fingers at his eyes and then back at Laurie and Bud in the universal symbol of "I'm watching you." Laurie couldn't believe he actually did that. It was so corny.

Besides, Laurie wasn't about to let it go that easily. "Yeah, but—" she started.

"No buts. Now get," Reginald barked, slapping at Laurie and Bud with his cleaning rag until they were forced to scurry away out of self-preservation.

Bud threw a look back over his shoulder as he dragged Laurie down the hallway. Reginald was standing, arms folded, in front of the door to the Tuckernuck bell tower. "I think getting that clue just got a lot more difficult."

Ways to Get Into the Locked Bell Tower
by Laurie Madison, grade six

1. Bust down the door by physical force.
   Problem: Need battering ram, and battering ram rentals not listed in Miss Lucille's ancient Yellow Pages or on Google.
2. Pick lock.
   Problem: Need skills. And lock-picking set. Also not in Yellow Pages.

3. Force Reginald to unlock door.
   Problem: Reginald hates us. Would definitely
   need some sort of weapon to force him,
   and would probably result in detention. Plus
   then secret's out.
4. Scale the wall from the outside.
   Problem: Noodle arms.
5. Mugging Reginald?
   Problem: Beginning of a life of crime.

EMAIL

FROM: WALKER LEFRANCO, School Board President
TO: PRINCIPAL MARTIN WINKLE, Tuckernuck Hall
SUBJECT: PATHETIC, WINKLE

It has come to my attention that there is to be
a Save Tuckernuck Hall rally. This is a pathetic
display of cheap sentimentality, Martin, and I
expect you to reign in your people ASAP. This
rally will only hurt your chances with the school
board.
—LEFRANCO

EMAIL

FROM: PRINCIPAL MARTIN WINKLE, Tuckernuck Hall

TO: WALKER LEFRANCO, School Board President

SUBJECT: Check your Constitution

Please note highlighted portion:

First Amendment—Congress shall make no
law respecting an establishment of religion,
or prohibiting the free exercise thereof; or
abridging the freedom of speech, or of the
press; **or the right of the people peaceably to
assemble,** and to petition the Government for a
redress of grievances.

EMAIL

FROM WALKER LEFRANCO, School Board President

TO PRINCIPAL MARTIN WINKLE, Tuckernuck Hall

SUBJECT: Principal LOON

You're as crazy as that Tutweiler woman was. Do
you know Picasso personally too?

Get a grip on reality, Winkle.

~

"Do I have to go?" Laurie looked in the mirror and adjusted her Clucker hat. She didn't know why she bothered, though. There was no way to make a chicken hat look fashionable, no matter how you arranged the dangling legs.

"Aren't you excited? It's your school! Don't you want to save it?" Mrs. Madison came into Laurie's room in full Clucker regalia—new hat, shirt, jacket, even an old Clucker pin she'd gotten when she went to school at Tuckernuck.

Laurie tried tying the legs over the top of her head like earflaps, but it wasn't a good look for the chicken or for her. "Wouldn't it be easier if I just switched to Hamilton? I mean, this rally. Is a rally really going to save the school? Really?" Laurie was skeptical.

Mrs. Madison hesitated. "We might be able to get the building designated as a historical landmark. Maria Tutweiler was rumored to have high-profile friends in the artistic community—Picasso, Alexander Calder, José de Creeft, Frank Lloyd Wright. Some people even say that there were famous artists and architects who helped with the renovations that turned Tuckernuck Hall into a school. Can you imagine demolishing a building like that?"

"But is that really true? I saw some articles—they said she was just crazy. That it's just an old building, and she didn't know anybody."

"A lot of people are looking for evidence to prove she wasn't crazy. I don't think she was."

Laurie couldn't help but notice that her mom hadn't really answered her questions. "And if it's a historic landmark, that'll save the school?"

Mrs. Madison bit her lip. "It'll save the building. And that's a start, right? One step at a time?" Mrs. Madison tugged on Laurie's ponytail and then smoothed her hair. "Let's get going, okay, kiddo? At least we're trying."

Laurie nodded, untied the chicken legs, and flung them back over her shoulders. What difference did it make? It was worth a shot if it would make Mom happy. And it's not like she'd see anyone there. Just other Cluckers, and they'd look as dumb as her.

Text message from Kimmy Baranski

R U at Rlly? I M!

"Laurie, is that you? Omigod, I can't believe it!"

Kimmy squealed and grabbed Laurie by the shoulders. "What is that thing on your head? I feel like I haven't talked to you in forever!"

Laurie squealed too, grabbing Kimmy in a huge hug. "I've missed you so much!"

Kimmy grinned. "I know! It's so weird not having you at Hamilton. Have you convinced your parents yet? Tell me you're starting next week."

Laurie shook her head and gave her mother a sidelong look. She was too far away to hear them. "Not yet. I'm still working on it though."

"What? That stinks, Laurie." Kimmy took a step back. "Didn't you ask your mom? Don't you want to go to the same school as me anymore?"

Laurie nodded so hard the chicken on her hat looked like a bobblehead. "Yeah, but it's complicated, see . . ."

"Nice hat." A girl with a sulky expression and a bushy brown ponytail appeared next to Kimmy and gave Laurie the once-over.

Laurie reached up and touched the chicken foot dangling over her shoulder self-consciously. "Yeah, well. It's a Clucker hat. I'm a Clucker. For now," she added as Kimmy frowned.

Kimmy pulled the ponytail girl forward. "Laurie, this

is Alyssa. She's like, my best Hamilton friend."

Laurie frowned. "Alyssa who smudged your shoes?"

Kimmy scowled. "That was a million years ago and a total accident, okay? Geez, I can't believe you brought that up."

"Nice to meet you too." Alyssa cracked her gum and rolled her eyes at Kimmy. "Nice friends, Kim."

"What? That's what you said!" Laurie didn't know what had happened, but the happy feeling between her and Kimmy was totally gone.

"Just drop it, okay? Geez." Kimmy shook her head at Laurie.

Laurie wished she'd never brought up the dumb shoes. But it wasn't like Kimmy had talked about much else. How was she supposed to know the shoe smudger was now her BFF and the whole shoe episode was totally off-limits?

"Laurie? Guess who I found!" Mrs. Madison called from somewhere in the crowd.

"Your mom's calling. Guess you'd better see what she wants." Kimmy toed the dirt with her pristine sneaker.

"Yeah. Call you later?" Laurie didn't want to leave things the way they were, but she didn't see how she could fix anything with Alyssa glaring at her.

"Sure. But I might be out." Kimmy wouldn't meet her

eyes. "They keep us pretty busy at Hamilton."

"It's a serious school," Alyssa said, eyeing Laurie's hat. "Not a lot of time for kid stuff, you know?" She reached out and inspected one of Laurie's chicken legs before dropping it again. "Come on, Kim."

Kimmy gave Laurie a helpless shrug as Alyssa pulled her away through the crowd. Laurie had a sick feeling in her stomach as she watched them leave. Everything that had to do with Kimmy seemed to give her a sick feeling these days.

Laurie flicked the chicken leg out of her face angrily. This whole Clucker thing could've been so fun if Kimmy was doing it too. How come Kimmy hadn't even tried to transfer to Tuckernuck? How come she had to be the one to switch?

"Laurie, there you are, you sneaky thing!" Mrs. Madison said, new chicken hat pushed back on her forehead. "Look who I found!"

Laurie looked up just in time to see her mother come through the crowd with Mr. Sanchez, the Keats fanatic. He was wearing a bright red Tuckernuck Cluckers shirt and a pair of turquoise shorts. With a chicken hat.

Laurie's mouth dropped open, but no words came out.

Mrs. Madison tweaked the brim of her Clucker hat.

"It's Bob Sanchez! Can you believe it? We were Cluckers at the same time! Isn't that great? Now, Laurie, I didn't know you were interested in English Romantic poetry!"

~

Note on refrigerator at the Wallace house

Horace Jr.:
Your head is in the clouds this week. Four errors on one quiz are four errors too many. Anyone can have a bad day, though. We'll redo the quiz when I get home from work Monday, and you can demonstrate you've mastered the material then.
(Also, when you asked to go to the chicken-themed rally, I could tell it was a joke, but I was tired and didn't "get it." Try telling it to me again tomorrow, okay? My sense of humor will be back then.)
Your father,
Horace Sr.

~

"Looks like somebody had a good night," Laurie said when Bud walked into homeroom the next day with a scowl on his face. Bud didn't respond; he just gave her a look that frosted the edges of her notebook.

"Yeah, me too." She sighed. "And I have no idea how we're getting past Reginald. Unless you count mugging him. That was my best idea."

Bud rolled his eyes and slammed himself down at his desk. "We're not mugging Reginald."

"I know. I'm just saying that was the best I could come up with." Laurie felt slightly insulted. Like she'd really planned on mugging Reginald. She didn't even own a ski mask.

"We'll get in there, no problem." Bud sighed. The last thing he felt like dealing with now was Laurie. His dad had given him another shot at taking his periodic table quiz after school, and he wasn't going to mess it up a second time.

"Well, sure," Laurie went on, oblivious. "I mean, of course we're getting in. I'm just saying we're going to have to be a little underhanded to do it, you know? Crafty."

Bud shook his head. Laurie was just a drama queen. "There are other ways to get things done than by being a total delinquent, okay? Let me handle it. I've got it covered."

Laurie snapped her mouth shut abruptly and turned to face the blackboard. Fine. If Bud had things so covered, she'd just leave it to him, since she was such a delinquent. And then when his big plan failed miserably, Laurie would swoop in and save the day. Now all she had to do was figure out how to do that.

IMPORTANT MESSAGE

FOR _Principal Winkle_

DATE _____ TIME_____ A.M. / P.M.

WHILE YOU WERE OUT

M _Horace Wallace Sr._

OF_____

PHONE NO. _____

TELEPHONED	✔	PLEASE CALL	✔
CALLED TO SEE YOU		WILL CALL AGAIN	
WANTS TO SEE YOU		RUSH	
	RETURNED YOUR CALL		

MESSAGE _Mr. Wallace is concerned that his son Horace Jr. (Bud) is becoming distracted from his studies and wants a meeting to make sure Horace Jr. (Bud) stays on track academically. (Also Flora brought doughnuts—_

SIGNED_they're in the staff room.)_

Thanks, Betty   PRINTED IN U.S.A.

Post-it on Betty Abernathy's computer monitor

WALLACE, AGAIN? GIVE ME
STRENGTH.
AND DO YOU KNOW HOW MANY
CALORIES ARE IN THOSE
DOUGHNUTS?
LEAD ME NOT INTO TEMPTATION,
BETTY.

MARTY

"So? What's the big plan?" Laurie hurried down the hallway after Bud, trotting to keep up. He'd refused to tell her anything about his plan, except that it was awesome, it was going to work no problem, and she shouldn't worry about it. Also that he was setting it into motion at lunch.

Laurie hoped whatever it was would work. Bud had been extra weird all day. And after the whole Kimmy encounter, all she wanted to do was find the treasure, become a superstar, and transfer. The search had already taken a lot longer than she had thought it would, and hanging around with Bud Wallace wasn't exactly working wonders on her (almost nonexistent) social life. Even Misti was starting to get irritated, and that was saying something.

Bud walked straight up to the front office and went inside, without even hesitating for a second. Laurie swallowed a yelp of surprise and hurried after him.

"Are you kidding me?" she whispered as he marched inside. "What, are you crazy?"

She was having serious doubts about taking Bud at his word now. It was obvious he'd completely flipped out and was going to spoil everything. Laurie bit her lip and tried to think positive thoughts. He wouldn't spill the beans, would he?

"Excuse me, ma'am?" Bud tapped his fingernails on the counter and tried to seem important and official.

Miss Abernathy, the office lady, didn't seem impressed by the act. Bud felt like turning around and going home. The whole treasure hunt was stupid anyway, especially when he could be doing something productive—like memorizing the dictionary pages he'd been assigned, maybe. Something useful.

Miss Abernathy finally turned around and flashed Bud a tight smile. "Yes?"

Bud's heart sank. At his old school he was Bud Wallace, honest and reliable A+ student (well, among the teachers, anyway). But Miss Abernathy barely knew him at all, and he could tell she wasn't going to roll over as easily as he'd hoped. Especially since she was flashing the "stop wasting my time, little man" smile. Still, it was worth a shot. He'd charmed enough office workers in his time. He would charm her. It was his gift.

"Miss Abernathy? Hi, I'm Bud Wallace." Bud smiled his most sincere and winning smile, the one that showed most of his teeth. "Reginald asked me to come get the key to the bell tower. He wants to get up there after lunch."

He smiled again and held out his hand expectantly.

Miss Abernathy's nose twitched like she smelled something bad. She narrowed her eyes slightly. "He sent you for the key?" she asked suspiciously.

"That's right," Bud said. "I was chatting with him, and he realized he didn't have it."

"Reginald. Reginald Moore sent you for the key? To the bell tower?"

"That's right." Bud felt his smile waver just a bit.

"Well, doesn't that just take the cake." She slammed her hand down on the counter with a smack. "I'm sorry, son, but if he's lost another key, that is not okay. Has he lost it, is that what you're saying?"

"No, uh . . . I mean . . ." Getting Reginald in trouble hadn't been the plan. It was time to backpedal, and fast.

"He didn't have the guts to tell me he'd lost the key? Is that it? Is that what we have here? A spineless miserable coward who sends a sixth grader to give me the bad news?"

"I . . . uh . . ." Bud opened and shut his mouth frantically, hoping that some plausible explanation would come out. But it didn't.

"Well, I'm not letting him get away with that." Miss Abernathy had gotten herself worked up in record time. She marched over to the intercom. "Let's just see what he has to tell me face-to-face, why don't we?"

Bud cringed as Miss Abernathy reached out to press the intercom button.

"Sheesh, Bud, way to get the message wrong." Laurie shot up to the desk and smacked him on the arm, hard. He turned to face her, wide-eyed. He had no idea what she was doing, but whatever it was, he hoped Miss Abernathy would buy it.

"What's that, hon?" Miss Abernathy's finger hovered a few millimeters away from the intercom button.

She'd stopped muttering curse words under her breath, so that was probably a good sign.

"Bud got it all wrong, is all." Laurie turned to Bud. "Reginald didn't *lose* the key, you moron. He's making a *new* key." She rolled her eyes and smiled at Miss Abernathy. "He said he wanted there to be lots of spare keys, just in case. He said he'd bring it to you for safekeeping when he did." She smacked Bud on the arm again. Bud thought she was overdoing it just a bit. "Way to get the message all backward." She shook her head at Miss Abernathy like Bud was the dumbest thing alive.

Miss Abernathy took her finger away from the intercom and smoothed her skirt. "Oh, is that all? Getting me all worked up." She gave an embarrassed laugh. "Thanks for the message. That's a good idea." She smiled at them and waved. "Bye now. And don't tell Reginald that I lost my temper, okay?"

"No problem." Laurie grabbed Bud by the shoulder and dragged him outside. Beads of sweat were forming on his forehead, and he looked like he might pass out.

"So that was the big idea?" Laurie asked when they were safely clear of the office.

"Pretty much," Bud said, leaning over and doing some deep breathing. The last thing he wanted to do was faint in the hallway.

"So I guess we go to plan B, huh?"

Bud nodded. "I guess so." He straightened up and frowned at Laurie. "Wait a minute, there's a plan B? What's plan B?"

Laurie just smiled.

Bud fiddled with the piece of duct tape and swore under his breath. He couldn't believe he'd let Laurie talk him into such a dumb plan. They were going to get caught for sure.

A little checking had shown that Reginald tended to go into the bell tower after school. (The little checking being Laurie finding out from her brother, Jack. Apparently Jack knew everything in the world and didn't ask that many questions. According to Laurie, at least. Bud hoped it was true.)

Sure enough, Reginald was pushing past kids in the hallway, making his way toward the bell tower door, just like Jack had said he would. Bud shrank back against the lockers, trying to be inconspicuous. He hoped Laurie would be able to pull off her part.

Laurie watched out of the corner of her eye as Reginald passed by. To a casual observer, it looked like she was just drinking from a plastic bottle of orange juice and having an animated discussion with Misti Pinkerton about the choreography for an official Clucker dance. The animated part was the key. And timing was everything.

Just as Reginald unlocked the bell-tower door and pulled it open, Laurie made her move. She raised the hand with the juice just as Misti waved her arms in an attempt to simulate vigorous arm flapping.

Bud had to hand it to her. If he hadn't known the whole thing was a setup, it would've looked like Misti was the one to smack into Laurie's arm, instead of the other way around.

Reginald turned just as Laurie dropped the bottle. He watched in horror as the arc of orange sprayed along the lockers on one side of the hallway and smashed onto the floor. And naturally, since this was junior high, the smashing sound was greeted with a hearty round of applause.

"Nooo!" Reginald howled, letting go of the door and dashing toward Laurie and the mess.

That was Bud's cue. Darting out of the shadows, he hurried up to the bell-tower door, grabbed it before it shut, and stuck the duct tape firmly in place over the inside of the lock. Then he quietly blended into the crowd.

The door to the bell tower closed, apparently locked, just as Laurie and Misti started apologizing profusely.

"I'm such a klutz, I'm so sorry!" Laurie pulled a wadded Kleenex out of her pocket and mopped at the spill.

Reginald waved his hands at her. "Get away! I'll take care of this. That's why drinks don't leave the cafeteria, you understand? I could write you up."

Laurie nodded, and blushing, she grabbed Misti Pinkerton's arm and hurried away.

"I'm so sorry about that, Laurie." Misti felt terrible. That's what she got for trying to dance. "I'm such a goober."

"It's fine," Laurie said, stifling a grin. "Trust me, it's not you. Let's just get out of here." She shot Bud a look of triumph as she hurried away.

New notice outside the cafeteria doors

REMEMBER, CLUCKERS
All food and drinks must be consumed while INSIDE the cafeteria. This will prevent nasty, sticky messes in classrooms and hallways.

NO EXCEPTIONS.
VIOLATIONS WILL RESULT IN DETENTION

Laurie and Bud leaned against the wall, trying to look inconspicuous. Sure, their plan had worked. Just not the way they'd thought.

"Is he still there?" Laurie whispered to Bud as he peeked around the hallway corner.

"Still there." Bud groaned. "He still has that mop and that little metal stool and everything."

Laurie checked her watch. After the whole spilled orange juice incident, Reginald had been patrolling the hallway with his mop and bucket at the ready. Halfway through the afternoon, he'd added the stool, so he could relax while monitoring for stray liquids. Laurie hadn't expected one spilled drink to hit him so hard. But apparently he took his job very seriously, and that hallway was now ground zero for liquid threats.

"I think we're going to have to call it a day," Bud said. "I can't miss the late bus."

Laurie nodded and tried not to think about how awful the weekend was going to be, waiting. She just hoped Reginald's hatred of all things liquid would keep him from noticing that duct tape. Because they weren't going to get a second chance.

Bud was arranging the cannons in his panorama of Valley Forge when Mr. Wallace came in. One cannon was in a central position, guarding the fort, another cannon was planning a distraction by dropping a bottle of juice, and the last cannon was about to save the day with a little handy duct-tape placement.

"Bud, look, I don't want to pry," his dad said after a minute, picking up one of the tiny cannons. "But is there anything you want to talk about?"

"What? No." Bud stood up abruptly.

"Nothing bothering you? Because you've seemed distracted lately." Mr. Wallace put the cannon back on the table, but on the other side of the Plasticine river. "Your cannon placement is off, and that's not like you."

"Oh, yeah, you're right. Sorry about that," Bud stammered, moving cannons across the river.

"Bud, forget the cannons. But you've been coming home late and leaving early, you're not concentrating, and I'm worried about you. Are you mixed up with some bad kids? You're not spending that time studying, I can tell that from the drills we've been doing."

Bud swallowed hard. He couldn't say anything about the treasure—that would just turn into a conversation about his mom, and all those conversations did was make everyone feel lousy.

"I don't know. I'm not really crazy about Valley Forge, I guess."

Mr. Wallace looked at him for a minute and then came over to him. Bud stiffened as his dad reached out and gave him an awkward hug.

"This isn't really about Valley Forge, is it."

Bud swallowed hard and shook his head.

"It's not easy with your mom gone," Mr. Wallace said, then let go and let his arms fall to his side. Bud stared at a cannon that had fallen into the river. "But remember what we decided? That we'd focus on your schoolwork and wouldn't let ourselves get distracted?"

Bud nodded. "I remember."

"Great." His dad smiled at him. "It's hard now, but it'll be worth it—you'll see." He took the cannon out of the river and set it upright. "I was thinking. I have some flexibility at work. What do you say I start driving you to and from school? Give us a little guy time. I could even quiz you on the way there."

Bud swallowed hard. "Sounds good." His heart sank. There went the extra treasure-hunting time. But his dad looked so happy with the idea, it wasn't like Bud was going to spoil it. "That'll be fun."

Bud's dad clapped him on the back. "Terrific. Now let's get this mess cleared up and have a little fun. You can explain the theories behind Washington's strategy to me. Sound good?"

—~—

"I think the coast is clear." Laurie pretended to tie her shoelace as she scanned the hallway. She'd been there so many times that day she was considering moving in. Maybe put a nice hammock over the lockers or something. She glared up at Bud. "You're sure you put the tape in the right place?"

"I think so." Bud scowled. He really hoped he had. He tried not to think about how much trouble he was going to be in if he missed the late bus. But he wasn't about to leave now, not with the next clue so close. His dad's buddy-time plan of driving him to and from school started tomorrow. And Reginald hadn't left the hallway all day, so who knew when they'd get another chance? Bud just hoped he hadn't noticed the tape.

"Then let's go." Laurie stood up, sauntered casually

over to the door, and taking a deep breath, jerked on the door. It opened.

—✐—

"Well, I guess we know what Reginald does in here, huh?" Bud said, pushing a discarded cigarette butt with his foot. There was a half-filled jar of cigarette butts, but even so, just as many seemed to have escaped and crawled onto the floor.

Laurie made a face and started up the curved wooden stairway. "Gross. Let's hurry up, okay?"

The bell tower was creeping her out. It was dark and musty smelling, like someone's basement or unused closet. Laurie glanced back to make sure Bud was following her and hurried up the steep stairway.

It wasn't what she expected. Laurie had pictured huge bells with cords that you could swing on, like they had in movies, but the bells all seemed to be attached to cords that went into an electronic-looking panel in the wall. No possibility of swinging there.

"I guess it's all computerized and electric now. That makes sense," Bud said. He scanned the room for anything that looked like a clue. If he was lucky, they'd find it fast, because this place was wreaking havoc on his sinuses.

Laurie barely glanced around her as she hurried up the stairs. She figured they'd check out the top first, and if they didn't find anything there, they could scope out the rest on the way out. She wasn't going to spend any extra time in this place, that was for sure.

Laurie came out on the platform that went around the bell tower and looked over the railing at the bells hanging in the center. However creepy the bell tower was, the bells were definitely impressive. They were all different sizes, but even the smallest was huge. They glowed dully in the light from the narrow windows overhead.

"Check it out, Bud. Aren't they awesome?" Laurie breathed. She couldn't believe they were hidden away where no one could see them.

"Yeah, they are." Bud took a step forward and looked closely at one of the bells. "And that's even more awesome." He pointed at one of the bells, his voice triumphant. "We did it, Laurie. It's got to be the next clue."

Laurie squinted at the bell. She could barely make out elaborate carving on the top and bottom of the bell. She gasped. They were words. The bell was inscribed with a quote.

"Get the notebook!" Laurie squealed, leaning forward as much as she dared to read the quotation. Which

wasn't that far, to be honest—that platform was pretty high up, and Laurie was feeling pretty homesick for the ground.

"It says, 'The church says the earth is flat...,'" Laurie said, inching around the platform as she read, "'... but I know that it is round.'" She craned her neck and then doubled back to look at the bell again. "That's it?"

"Check the next one," Bud said, writing furiously.

Laurie moved farther along the platform and squinted at the biggest bell. "You're right! Okay, on top this one says, 'For I have seen the shadow on the moon . . .'" She hunched down to read the bottom part of the bell. "'. . . and I have more faith in a shadow than in the church.'"

"Got it," Bud said, wishing he'd sharpened his pencil after sixth period. "Next?"

Laurie moved down the platform to the smallest bell. "This one just has a big H on it."

"H. Got it." Bud nodded. "Anything on the last one?"

Laurie squinted at the last bell. It was the farthest away, and she was having trouble reading it. "It looks like . . . Shak . . . got it! Shakespeare!"

Bud dropped the pencil. "Shakespeare? Really?"

"Shakespeare! The quote must be from one of his plays!" Laurie suppressed an urge to jump up and down.

She'd wait and do that when they got back on solid ground.

"That's got to be it." Bud whistled. "This is awesome. You know what that means? It means the next clue's in the theater."

"It's got to be!" Laurie hurried over to Bud and bobbed nervously up and down in place.

Bud stared at her bobbing. Finally he caved. "What are you doing?"

"You're blocking the stairs, Bud. Move it! Come on, hustle." Laurie felt like she'd explode if she didn't get out of that bell tower. Apparently she had a teeny weeny fear of heights. Who knew?

Bud nodded and hurried down the stairs. He was glad this was an easy one. They'd hit the theater, find the next clue, and hopefully get the treasure. It was all going to be smooth sailing ahead.

PART FIVE

SEARCHING THE WORLD

"Do you think we should figure out which play it's from?" Laurie asked as they hurried toward the theater. Bud was acting like they were on some kind of deadline or something. Something was definitely up with him.

Bud shook his head. "It's fine, it's a play, it's in the theater, we'll find it. Probably backstage or something. Let's go."

They turned the corner and ran toward the doors of Reynolds Auditorium.

AUDITIONS TODAY!
For this year's musical production,
Billy and the Pirates!
Needed: Dancers! Singers! Actors!
Pirates! Everyone!

"Oh, no. Forget it," Bud said, screeching to a halt in front of the theater. "You're not getting me in there."

Laurie groaned. "Come *on*. It's not like you'll get cast as a pirate or anything. They won't make you audition."

Bud shook his head. "Right. Just like they didn't make me second tenor. Not on your life."

Laurie sighed and looked around. "How about we go the backstage way, then? We pretty much checked out the seat area before, anyway. We'll peek around back-stage, quiet as mice, and they'll never spot us. Okay? We'll be in and out with that clue before they know what hit them."

Bud glared at her. "Fine. But if they see us, it's all you. You're the pirate. Not me. Got it?"

Laurie nodded. "Sure. No problem. I'll take the bullet if we get caught." She shrugged. Bud was making way too big a deal out of the whole thing. It wasn't like any-one was going to notice them.

Laurie and Bud plodded out of the theater along with a surge of other kids. They'd searched all over the back-stage area, but there was nothing. No random letter, no quote, no bust of Shakespeare, nothing that seemed remotely connected to the quote on the bells. The whole search had been a washout.

Bud flopped down onto the floor by the auditorium. Laurie slumped next to him.

"That was so not worth it." Bud groaned. "That was so so so not worth it."

Laurie smacked him on the arm. But it was a half-hearted attempt at best. Bud didn't even seem to notice. "Stuff it," she said. "At least you didn't have to yo ho ho."

"True." Bud didn't even have the heart to argue. "Your yo ho ho was good, though."

"Don't even."

After a few minutes, Miss Downey came out of the auditorium and pinned a piece of paper to the wall. Laurie and Bud waited until the rest of the kids had drifted away before looking at it.

"Great." Bud sighed. "I'm Pirate Cook. How about you?"

Laurie didn't answer; she just thunked her head against the wall.

Bud checked the list. "Well, look on the bright side," he said. "How many lines can Polly the Parrot have?"

EMAIL

FROM: OLIVIA HUTCHINS, Tuckernuck Hall

TO: PRINCIPAL MARTIN WINKLE, Tuckernuck Hall

SUBJECT: Still No Magic Bullet

Just to keep you in the loop—I still haven't located any evidence that any famous artists or architects contributed to the renovation or construction at Tuckernuck Hall. It does seem that Mrs. Tutweiler and many of the artists and architects in question were in the same regions at the same time, but whether they even knew each other is unclear.

I wish I had better news for you. I'm going to keep working, though, and hope to have something substantial for you before the school board meets this week.

Thanks,

Olivia

"So what do you think? Try searching again?" Bud and Laurie stood outside the auditorium, pretending to look at the casting sheet again. Laurie shuddered. Like she wanted to relive the horror. At least she hadn't gotten cast in one of the killer rat roles—that was the only silver lining to the whole ordeal. That honor went to Calliope and Mariah Jeffries, neither of whom seemed very pleased with their new roles, if Mariah's watery red eyes and scowl were any indication. Like it really made a difference, though. Laurie had a feeling *Billy and the Pirates!* was one weird play.

"I think we'd be better off identifying the quote. The play is probably the important part."

"I bet you're right," Bud said. He had a feeling that as

Pirate Cook, he was going to be pretty sick of that auditorium before long, so he might as well keep his distance while he could. "Library?"

Laurie nodded and headed down the hall.

Miss Lucille knitted her eyebrows and gave them a sad wave when they came in. She seemed to think they were still broken up over the whole Mrs. Reynolds thing. Laurie put on her sad clown face and waved back.

Troy Hopkins was hogging the internet computer when they got there, but thankfully it only took a few minutes of obnoxious hovering and intense, unblinking staring before he felt uncomfortable enough to log off and slink away. Bud gave Laurie the thumbs up, hopped on to the computer, and whipped out his notebook.

"Okay, here we go. 'The church says the earth is flat . . . ,'" he said out loud as he typed. He smirked at Laurie. "My good friend Google should have the play for us in just a sec," he said as he finished typing. "And voilà!" Bud pushed enter with a flourish.

"And it's from . . . huh."

Laurie craned her neck to see, but the glare on the screen made it hard to read. "What? What's it from?"

Bud frowned. "It's not from a play. It's not even

Shakespeare. It's Magellan."

Laurie made a face. "Magellan? *The* Magellan? The explorer?"

"Yeah, weird, huh? See, it says right here. The quote is from Ferdinand Magellan, first man to—"

His eyes got wide, and he looked up at Laurie.

"Circumnavigate the globe!" They said in unison.

Bud did a fist pump. "To the science wing! It's something about the planets, right?"

Laurie put her fingers to her temples. "No, wait—the Globe . . . I just saw something about that. Somewhere. In the . . . in the English wing! That weirdo English teacher had a poster!"

"You're right, that's it! That's the connection between Magellan and Shakespeare." Bud gloated.

"The Globe was Shakespeare's theater." Laurie did a little happy dance. But discreetly, since she was in a library and all.

"Right!"

Laurie stopped dancing. "Except it's obviously not the real Shakespeare's Globe. She couldn't expect us to go to England."

"Of course not. We just need to find the right globe," Bud said, a little too loudly. He had definitely forgotten to use his library voice.

"Globe? Right over there, dear." Miss Lucille nodded as she hurried by. Mariah Jeffries was browsing through the books in the stacks, glancing at each one and dropping the rejects onto the floor. Apparently she was still in full sulk mode. Miss Lucille had her work cut out for her.

Bud and Laurie turned in the direction that Lucille had pointed, and sure enough, there in the corner was an enormous antique globe.

"Check it out," Bud said. "How awesome is that?"

Laurie barely heard him. She was already making a beeline for the globe and was halfway across the room by the time Bud had gotten away from the computer.

"This has got to be it," Laurie breathed as she looked at the enormous old globe. It was in a floor stand that took up the entire corner of the room. There were tiny drawings of sea serpents and jumping fish in the oceans, and the names of all of the continents were written in elaborate old-fashioned script. Laurie was almost afraid to touch it, it looked so fancy.

Bud didn't waste any time worrying about touching it, though. His hands were all over that globe in two seconds flat. Without hesitating for a moment, he spun the globe on its axis, looking for Maria Tutweiler's next clue.

The globe gracefully turned in a full circle, and Bud and Laurie leaned forward to inspect every word and drawing. When it was done, Bud spun it gently again. And again.

Bud had gone past Brazil ten times before Laurie put her hand out and stopped him. "I don't think it's written on the globe, Bud. It's somewhere else."

Bud frowned. She was probably right. Sure, it was pretty and fancy, but none of the pictures or writing looked like anything but regular globe stuff. Besides, all that spinning was making him vaguely nauseous.

"Maybe it's inscribed? On the base, maybe?" Laurie squatted down and inspected the base of the globe. But all she saw was the dull shine of brushed nickel—no inscriptions, no symbols, nothing.

Laurie sighed and toppled back onto her butt. "I don't see it." She felt like she'd been saying that a lot lately.

"Me neither." Bud stood, hands on hips, glaring at the globe. He knew this was the right solution to the puzzle. It had to be. But for the life of him, he couldn't figure out what he was supposed to find.

Laurie scooched forward and took over the random globe spinning for a while. But no matter how many times the globe circled its axis, no secret messages magically appeared.

"Huh." Laurie looked up at Bud. "What do you think?"

"Beats me," Bud said. "Maybe it's underneath?" He shot a look at Miss Lucille, who had gotten Mariah under control and was now happily picking fuzzy pilled places off of her sweater. "Help me tilt it."

Laurie grabbed the base of the globe stand, and Bud grabbed the top. Working as a team, they tried to wrestle the globe onto its side. But despite their best efforts, they only managed to tilt it a few centimeters off of the ground.

"Quick . . . look . . . under . . . ," Bud grunted, holding the globe stand at an angle. His face started turning a pretty scary shade of dark pink.

Laurie lay flat and peered under the globe, but she couldn't see anything except a big circular dent in the carpet and some random pieces of linty dust. "Nothing." She shook her head.

"Feel . . . around . . ." Bud looked like he was about to burst a vein in his forehead. "Under."

Laurie looked at him doubtfully. He wasn't going to be able to hold that thing much longer, and the last thing she wanted to do was lose a hand. She shot a look at Miss Lucille, but Miss Lucille was still blissfully unaware that her library globe was being manhandled.

"Reach . . . under!" Bud gasped.

"There's nothing there, Bud," Laurie said. "Trust me. I don't need to feel around."

Bud finally dropped the globe with a thunk. "You're sure? You didn't find anything?"

Laurie looked up guiltily. "Nope. Nothing." At least she was pretty sure there was nothing under there. Nothing they could reach, anyway.

Mariah Jeffries shoved her chair back from the library table and stomped out, narrowly missing stepping on Laurie's fingers. Laurie wasn't sure whether the missing part was intentional or not, but she did know one thing. She'd been a Tuckernuck Clucker for what, two weeks? And she'd already managed to (a) make new enemies and (b) come across like a complete loony tune. Forget Kimmy—at this rate she'd have to transfer just to keep from being a complete social outcast.

"You okay?" Bud flexed his fingers sympathetically. "Still have all your parts?"

Laurie snorted and waggled her fingers back at him. Maybe not a complete social outcast. At least she'd have company.

~

"Maybe it's a different globe? Who else has a globe?"

Bud stood in the middle of the history hallway and looked thoughtful. Laurie didn't feel thoughtful. They'd been in a million classrooms so far and looked at three different globes, and every one was vying for the title of most boring globe ever. No clues, nothing.

They'd even tried the science hall, but it had been a total bust. The theme there seemed to be more star oriented, and the constellations painted on the ceiling there were cool to look at but not helpful at all. The history hall was the last one left to check.

Laurie's eyes darted around the hallway, and she worked her hands the way that Ponch and Jon did when they were anxious. "I can't get roped into any more extracurriculars, Bud."

"Yeah, tell me about it," Bud said. He pointed at a carving up on the molding near the ceiling. "Is that a globe?"

Laurie peered up at the carving. "That's Abraham Lincoln. Not a globe."

"Shoot." Bud slumped. "And that's not a globe?" He pointed at a carving on the opposite side of the hallway.

"Random founding father, I think," Laurie said.

"Not a globe. We've been through this." It had been a long day.

Bud dropped his book bag down at his feet. "Maybe it is a Shakespeare thing? We didn't really try that."

"Whatever, we just need to get out of here." She'd spotted a shadow behind one of the stained-glass panels in one of the classroom doors. And shadows meant one thing—teachers.

She grabbed Bud by the arm, not even worrying about bruising, and dragged him out into the main hallway. It was amazing how much more relaxed she felt away from the specialized wings.

Bud trudged along behind her for a few steps and then stopped. "If it's Shakespeare, you know where we have to go."

"I know." Laurie chewed her lip and thought hard. She was going to have to nip that whole English hall problem in the bud. It might as well be now. "Okay. I have an idea." She grinned at Bud. "I think this just may work."

Laurie set off down the hallway and turned deliberately, right into the English wing. Bud gasped. She hadn't even checked for Mr. Sanchez. Whatever she was planning, Bud sure hoped it would work. He wasn't going to another poetry club for moral support. He had his music to think of.

—✗—

"Why, Laurie, what a nice surprise!" Mr. Sanchez got up as Laurie marched into the room. "Is this about the Keats club? I was thinking we could have some of those English butter crackers for snacks, but I'm not locked into anything. It's just an idea."

Laurie nodded. "Butter crackers sound great, but I have to talk to you. About Keats."

Mr. Sanchez leaned against his desk. "Yes?"

Laurie shifted her weight from foot to foot. "It's just . . . well, I've been thinking, and I think I want to keep my love of Keats private right now."

"Private. I see." Mr. Sanchez frowned.

Laurie nodded. "It's personal, you know. My personal connection with the poetry. I'm just not ready to share that yet. Emotionally."

"I see." Mr. Sanchez was really frowning now. "Not even with other like-minded students?"

Laurie shook her head. "It would make it less special?"

"Hmm. Less special," Mr. Sanchez echoed. Laurie knew she had to act quickly or her plan would all fall apart.

"So I wanted to ask you about Shakespeare. That's really why I came. Is there a lot of Shakespeare stuff around the school? About his theater, the Globe? Or anything?"

"Nothing that I'm aware of, unfortunately. Why? Were you hoping to do a segment on Shakespeare instead? Is that not too painful to share? Emotionally?"

Laurie shot Mr. Sanchez a suspicious look, but he seemed dead serious.

Laurie shrugged. "Well, not exactly. I just thought I'd see if focusing on Shakespeare might help with my . . . uh . . . Keats issues."

Mr. Sanchez's frown started to go away. "I see."

"I don't want you to do anything, okay? Seriously. I'm just curious," Laurie said quickly.

Mr. Sanchez stroked his beard in his creepy way and nodded slowly. "There are some nice volumes of Shakespeare in the library. You might take a look at those. But I'll put my thinking cap on. And thank you, Laurie. I appreciate your candor."

"Any time." Laurie smiled. She felt like skipping. She'd handled that like a pro—no more Sanchez problems for her.

～

Bud was humming quietly to himself when Laurie came up behind him. He was really into it and didn't even notice when she came screeching to a stop and dropped her mouth open. She had to do it three times before he stopped humming and looked up.

"What?"

"Excuse me, but were you . . ." Laurie narrowed her eyes and cocked her head. "No, I'm sorry. I must be mistaken. It almost sounded like you were . . . humming."

Bud rolled his eyes. "Stuff it, Laurie."

"I know, I must be hallucinating. It sounded like, I don't know, choral music of some sort?"

Bud's ears turned bright red.

"Are you actually *enjoying chorus*?" Laurie poked him in the side. "Something you want to tell me, Bud? Any deep, dark musical confessions?"

"Like you haven't been humming that 'Yo Ho Ho' song from *Billy and the Pirates!*, Polly," Bud said, trying not to grin.

Laurie grinned back and flopped down into a chair. "Well, I had a little heart-to-heart with my ol' buddy Sanchez. He said there are some Shakespeare books in the library we should check out."

Now it was Bud's turn to drop his jaw. "Sanchez? You

talked to him? What the heck?"

Laurie shrugged. "Didn't I mention? My Sanchez problems are OVER."

Notice on the English hall bulletin board

EXCITING NEW CLUB!
By Popular Demand,
The English Department will start the very first SHAKESPEARE CLUB!
Connect emotionally with the Bard!
Meetings, Wednesdays after school
WITH SNACKS!
Sign up with Mr. Sanchez, room 212.

Note from Calliope to Secret School Source

I think I've figured out a way to find out what Laurie Madison and Bud Wallace are up to. It's got to be related to the treasure. This could be big.
Will report soon.
Calliope

Note from Flora Downey to Bud Wallace

> Bud,
> I still haven't received your signed
> permission slips. I need to have them
> by the end of the week if you're going to
> participate in any extracurricular activities.
> Thank you,
> Miss Downey

Note from Horace Wallace Jr. to Horace Wallace Sr.

> Dad, I know what we decided about
> extracurriculars, but could you sign this
> permission slip? It's kind of required. Miss
> Downey wants me to do it—she says it'll help
> me look well-rounded for colleges. I won't let it
> affect my grades.
> Thanks,
> Bud

Laurie pulled out her notebook and stared at her list. She and Bud had inspected every volume of Shakespeare in the library but hadn't found a thing except a math test from 2003 and a squished bug of an undetermined species.

"Okay, we need to do some word association. Brainstorming. Globe. What comes to mind? Besides real globes and Shakespeare and a theater in England we're not going to."

"Nothing. Nothing comes to mind," Bud grumbled. He pointed to the huge globe in the corner of the library. "This is the globe. We're just missing it. We're just too stupid to see the clue."

Laurie rolled her eyes. "We've been over this, Bud. There's nothing to miss." She glared at the huge globe, just sitting there taunting them. "Except . . ."

Bud perked up. "Except what?"

Laurie got up and squatted down next to the globe. Then she reached out and ran her fingers along the brushed nickel base. She frowned. "Does this look new to you?"

Bud gave a short, barky laugh. "New? It's an ancient globe, Laurie. Yeah, real new."

"He's right, dear. It's a very old globe," Miss Lucille said, hurrying over, adjusting her sweater. "It was in Maria Tutweiler's family for years." She took a soft cloth out of her pocket and started rubbing the globe stand carefully. Apparently she couldn't take Laurie's grubby paws messing up the finish.

"Well, I know that," Laurie said grumpily, getting to her feet. "I just meant the base looked new."

"Oh, you're right, dear. It's a very new base." Miss Lucille beamed at them both. "Isn't it fun when everybody's right?"

"What?" Bud said, straightening up. "It's new? Really? How new?"

"Oh, yes. There was an incident a few years back." Miss Lucille leaned in and whispered conspiratorially. "Roughhousing." She raised her eyebrows at them like she'd just said a dirty word. "It was damaged. And the school board felt that this one looked more modern and stylish. It's a shame, though. The old stand was very distinctive."

"Distinctive how?" Laurie held her breath. "Was it inscribed or something?"

"Oh, yes, such pretty letters too. Of course I can't remember what it said, but it was a lovely piece." Miss Lucille gave a tinkly laugh, like not remembering was no big deal. Laurie wanted to throttle her.

"Are you sure you can't remember?" Laurie begged. "Maybe just a little?" She resisted the urge to clutch at

Miss Lucille's arm. She didn't want to spook her.

Miss Lucille put on her thinking face for a moment; then she brightened up again. "No. No, I'm sorry. I've drawn a blank, unfortunately." She laughed again.

Laurie's face fell. She couldn't believe they'd come that far just to hit a dead end. "Oh. Okay."

Miss Lucille patted Laurie on the head like she was a puppy. "Of course, if it's important, we could just go look, couldn't we?"

"Could we?" Laurie said, hardly able to breathe.

"Well, yes, of course. I believe it's in the prop room. They used it for one of their musical productions a few years back. Some horrible play about the apocalypse, I believe. But with pirates. So that cheered it up a bit."

EMAIL

FROM: PRINCIPAL MARTIN WINKLE, Tuckernuck Hall
TO: FLORA DOWNEY, Tuckernuck Hall
SUBJECT: HORACE WALLACE JR. EXTRACURRICULARS

Miss Downey,
I understand that Horace Wallace Jr. is a member of the sixth-grade chorus and a participant in this year's production of *Billy*

and the Pirates! However, I have spoken with his father, and Horace Jr. is only to be involved in extracurricular activities that are academic in nature. Mr. Wallace met with me today and is adamant that his son not be required to participate in the chorus or in any theatrical pursuits, so if Horace Jr. attempts to rehearse or join in chorus activities, please send him to speak with me.

Thank you,

Martin Winkle

EMAIL

FROM: FLORA DOWNEY, Tuckernuck Hall

TO: PRINCIPAL MARTIN WINKLE, Tuckernuck Hall

SUBJECT: Excuse Me?

Marty,

Chorus isn't academic? Who says?

Flora

EMAIL

FROM: PRINCIPAL MARTIN WINKLE, Tuckernuck Hall

TO: FLORA DOWNEY, Tuckernuck Hall

SUBJECT: My Hands are Tied

Flora,

Mr. Wallace says. I'm sorry, but it's not up to us. We have to comply with his wishes.

Marty

EMAIL

FROM: FLORA DOWNEY, Tuckernuck Hall

TO: PRINCIPAL MARTIN WINKLE, Tuckernuck Hall

SUBJECT: Ha!

We'll see about that.

Bud and Laurie waited until Miss Lucille was deep in discussion with old Mr. Murphy, the band director, before they rushed to inspect the old cracked globe stand. Once they'd gotten to the prop room, Miss Lucille realized she didn't have the key, so she'd had to track down Mr. Murphy for help. Laurie was glad that she did, because even though that meant that the walk back to the prop room took ten times as long, it also meant she and Bud had at least a few minutes alone with the stand while Miss Lucille and Mr. Murphy reminisced about the good old days thirty thousand years ago.

"Well, this is it, all right," Laurie said, bending over the frame and smiling. "Check it out." Laurie pointed at the curve of metal that used to hold the globe in place. Carved deep into the metal was an elaborate letter I.

"And look." Bud wiped a clear patch in the dust on the base of the stand. "This is it. Laurie, this is it."

Using the edge of his shirt, he wiped the base clean, revealing the inscription there. TEMPUS AD LUCEM DUCIT VERITATEM.

Laurie did a little happy dance in place. "We did it!" She looked at the inscription again. "I just wish I knew what it said!"

Bud already had his notebook out and was copying it down. He paused for a second and smiled at her. "It's Latin," he said. "And if there's one thing I know, it's Latin."

Letter from Flora Downey to Horace Wallace Sr.

Dear Mr. Wallace:

I was sorry to hear that you wish to have your son, Bud, resign his position as second tenor in the sixth-grade chorus. I understand that you are concerned that participating in music study will somehow take away from his academic work.

I have taken the liberty of attaching a study published in the March 1999 issue of the scientific journal *Neurological Research* that suggests that students exposed to musical training have more highly developed math skills than students with no musical training. Students who study music have higher scores on standardized tests and have a greater understanding of ratios, fractions, proportions, and thinking in space and time. They are also less likely to drop out of school.

I am sure that you would not intentionally damage your son's math education in any way. Therefore, I will expect to see him at chorus and musical

*theater rehearsals for the remainder of the
semester.*

Yours sincerely,

Flora Downey

Misti looked up as Laurie set her lunch tray down on the table. "Where's Bud?"

"What?" Laurie slid into her seat sulkily.

"You know, your shadow? Remember him?" Misti took a bite of her celery. "Aren't you guys, like, best buds now or something?"

Laurie rolled her eyes. "I told you, it's just a project. It's not like we're friends or anything. Sheesh." She didn't feel like talking about it. Bud hadn't met her before school, and he hadn't even spoken to her in homeroom. It was like he was ignoring her.

"And besides, I'm not his keeper. I don't know where he is." Laurie glared at Misti, who was just watching her, noisily munching her celery. "Hey, you don't know Latin, do you?"

Misti frowned at Laurie like she'd gone insane. "Uh, no?" She took another big crunch of celery. "You're in a mood," she said with her mouth full.

Laurie just shrugged. If Misti thought she was in a mood now, she should just wait. If Bud thought he could get that treasure without her just because he knew Latin and she didn't, he had another think coming. She couldn't believe she'd actually trusted him.

Laurie pushed her tray of congealing fish sticks away. The smell was making her stomach revolt. Then she pulled out her science notebook and started doodling in the margin of one of the pages. She'd already doodled a big D, A, and H, and now she started to add the I. She and Bud had been pretty much ignoring the letters that appeared with the clues, but they had to be there for a reason.

"So have you memorized your lines yet?" Misti crunched her way through another piece of celery.

Laurie looked confused. "Lines for what?"

"Duh. Polly the Parrot? You're onstage a lot." Misti grinned.

Laurie groaned. "Yeah, I got right to work on that. 'Polly wants a cracker' is so hard to remember." That was the only line she had in the whole play, except for in the big dance number, where she had to flap her arms and squawk periodically.

Misti giggled. "It's better than 'Grr . . . grr . . . grrow-wwl,' which is what Calliope and Mariah have to say."

Laurie smirked and doodled on the notebook again. A . . . H . . . D . . . I. "That's true. And I don't have to wear that scary mouse nose-and-teeth combo."

"Mariah's going to look great in that," Misti said. "Remind me to bring my camera."

Laurie smacked Misti playfully on the arm. She didn't need Bud. She'd figure out that Latin stuff without him. All she needed was a computer with internet anyway, right? She doodled big, elaborate letters down the middle of the page. I . . . H . . . A . . . D . . .

Misti glanced at the paper. "What?"

Laurie looked up. "What?"

Misti pointed at the notebook. "You had what?"

Laurie looked down at the letters she'd just written in the notebook. I HAD. "Holy cow, Misti. That's it."

"What? What's it?"

Laurie shoved her notebook back into her book bag. "I'll explain later. I've got to find Bud!"

She'd find him and they'd figure the whole thing out. But Bud or no Bud, there was no way she was giving up the hunt now.

Bud sat in the library, staring at his math book. He had to finish the worksheet page for his dad, but his heart

wasn't in it. He kept thinking of that Latin phrase—
TEMPUS AD LUCEM DUCIT VERITATEM. If he could just
figure out that clue . . .

Bud pushed the thought out of his mind and stared at
the fractions on his worksheet. It didn't matter what that
clue led to, it wasn't like he was going to be able to find
the next one, not now that his dad had started the whole
"guy time" thing. Door-to-door driving service, that's
what he called it, but what it basically meant was that he
dropped Bud off right before the first bell and picked
him up right after the final bell. No time to loiter around
school and get mixed up with a bad crowd. Actually, no
time to get mixed up with a crowd at all.

Bud sighed and stared at the numbers on the paper in
front of him. He hadn't even had the guts to go into the
cafeteria for lunch. He didn't want to see Laurie's face
when he broke the news that his treasure-hunting days
were pretty much over.

"Ahem."

Bud's stomach dropped. Like he'd really have been
able to avoid Laurie. She glared at him from the other
side of the table, arms folded.

Bud gave a weak smile. "Oh. Hey."

"So, making yourself scarce, huh?"

Bud shrugged. "Got a lot to do."

Laurie slid into a seat opposite him. "Don't even think you're going to find that treasure without me, Bud. Because I've got a vital piece of the clue you're totally missing."

Bud didn't know what the heck she was talking about. "What clue? I'm the one who knows Latin, okay? And that clue's in Latin."

Laurie just smirked. "Right. Now you tell me what it means, and *maybe* I'll tell you my clue."

Bud frowned and closed his math workbook. It would be fine. He wouldn't get caught up in the search, he would just tell her the translation and be done with it. Maybe do a little brainstorming. That was it. Nothing wrong with that.

He pulled out the piece of paper with the Latin phrase. "Okay, '*Tempus ad lucem ducit veritatem*'? So *tempus*, that means time, right? And *veritatem*, that's truth or truthfulness."

Laurie nodded. "Okay, so time truthfulness? What's the rest? What does it mean?"

"It's . . . time brings . . . time brings truth to light." Bud sighed in satisfaction. He never thought he'd be so glad his dad had made him study Latin.

"It sounds like an ad. For a watch or a lightbulb or something," Laurie scoffed. "Are you sure you got it right?"

"Time brings truth to light," Bud continued, ignoring her. He was so done with her. "So it's got to be something with light or time—maybe a lamp or skylight or something. Or if it's time . . . shoot, what if it's something happening at a specific time? That's going to stink because we've missed it by what, eighty years?"

Laurie shook her head. "She wouldn't do that. It wouldn't be something we could miss. She didn't know when people would figure it out."

Bud stared at the clue like the words were going to jump up and explain themselves. "Maybe something that happens every day?"

Laurie nodded. "Or maybe something else. Maybe lamp is right. Or a clock?"

Bud grinned. "A clock sounds good. I bet it's a clock." He felt a pang at the idea of Laurie finding the next clue without him, but he pushed it away.

Laurie grinned back. She could've totally figured it out without Bud, but it was nice not to have to work it all out herself.

"So what's your big clue?" Bud asked skeptically. He

almost didn't ask, since it was obvious that had all been a bluff, but he figured it wouldn't hurt to put her on the spot a little.

Laurie just grinned wider. Bud felt a shadow of doubt creep in.

She pulled out a really ratty-looking notebook filled with scrawls. Pretty pathetic work for so early in the year, Bud thought, but who was he to judge, right? Laurie tapped on the big scribbled letters in the middle of the page.

Bud glanced at it. "I had? I had what?"

Laurie tapped on the page again. "D . . . A . . . H . . . I. Ring any bells, Bud? So to speak." If she grinned any more, her head was going to split in two.

"Um, no, I don't—" Bud stopped suddenly. "D-A-H-I?" he whispered.

"That's right." Laurie slapped the notebook shut.

"I HAD. Okay then." Bud smiled. He couldn't help himself—he was impressed. And he wasn't about to give up now. "We are so going to find that treasure."

PART SIX

TIME WAITS FOR NO ONE

"I'm thinking it's not a classroom clock," Laurie said as she scooped up Ponch (or Jon) and quickly shoved him in a shoe box with Jon (or Ponch) so Bud could change the cedar chips. She patted the top of the box in satisfaction. One thing Laurie could say for Mrs. Hutchins's classroom duties—she'd definitely figured out a couple of important gerbil-related facts.

IMPORTANT GERBIL-RELATED FACTS
by Laurie Madison, grade six

1. They are very small, much smaller than a motivated human.
2. They are not more afraid of you than you are of them, so watch your back at all times.
3. They can be distracted by many things, mostly food related, no matter how disgusting.
4. If you grab them quickly from behind, they don't have time to prepare for war.

One small piece of apple from the school's vending machine, and it was all over for the evil duo. And their tiny fists were no match for a closed shoe box.

"Probably not a wall clock, you're right," Bud agreed, completely missing the whole gerbil-related drama unfolding before him. "And there's not a single skylight in this stupid school."

"And I don't think the fluorescent overhead lights are what she meant either," Laurie said. "So after this, we'll go through room by room. It's sure to be somewhere."

Bud looked up nervously. "Uh. Yeah, about that. I can't this afternoon. I have to get home."

Laurie's ears pricked up. Something was definitely going on with him. "Oookay. You can't stay even a little late?"

Bud shook his head. "Nope. Sorry."

"Tomorrow before school, then?" Laurie tried to keep her tone pleasant. It wouldn't be very diplomatic to let on that she was itching to pummel him.

Bud finished filling the gerbil cage with fresh cedar chips and unceremoniously emptied the rodent pair back into their cage. Ponch and Jon immediately leaped to their feet, spoiling for a fight, but their tiny curses fell on deaf ears. "Sorry, no," Bud finally said, putting the lid on the cage.

"Lunchtime?" Laurie couldn't believe her ears. Pummeling was too good for Bud.

"Sure, okay," Bud said, avoiding Laurie's eyes. "We'll figure it out then."

Bud grabbed his book bag and was out of the door before Laurie managed to pick up her jaw off of the floor.

EMAIL
FROM: PRINCIPAL MARTIN WINKLE
TO: OLIVIA HUTCHINS
SUBJECT: Crossing my Fingers

I'm leaving for the meeting now, but I thought I'd check one last time. Anything for me?

EMAIL
FROM: OLIVIA HUTCHINS
TO: PRINCIPAL MARTIN WINKLE
RE: Crossing my Fingers

I'm really sorry. There's just nothing there.

School Board Meeting Minutes

1. School board president Walker LeFranco called the meeting to order.
2. The board approved minutes for the meeting held last month, in August.
3. The board honored last year's retirees.
4. Land developer Bruno Baker presented statistics showing that the property on Shadyway Lane (currently occupied by Tuckernuck Hall Intermediate School) would be valued at ten times its current value if sold immediately as commercial property. A generous offer is on the table.
5. Walker LeFranco asked the president of the Save Tuckernuck group to present definitive evidence of historical importance.
6. Minimal evidence was cited and was deemed to be insufficient.
7. People in chicken shirts called to order.
8. LeFranco called for vote to close Tuckernuck and sell property immediately.
9. People in chicken shirts escorted out for disorderly conduct.
10. Resolution passes. Tuckernuck Hall

will close as soon as students can be
integrated into neighboring schools,
namely Hamilton Junior High and Savannah
Heights Middle School.
11. Meeting adjourned.
Minutes compiled by Acting Secretary
Terry Ailiff

Post-it attached to minutes
*From Acting Secretary Terry Ailiff, to Janet Brown, Committee
Records Supervisor*

You would not BELIEVE the
ruckus at tonight's school
board meeting. I thought
that LeFranco and Winkle
were going to rip each
other's throats out over the
Tuckernuck school closing!
I haven't seen such a fuss
since LeFranco banned
sweets in the schools.
                          Terry

Laurie was watching a show about dog detectives on Animal Planet when her dad stormed in and threw his Clucker hat on the chair.

"Well, looks like you get your wish, Laurie." He cussed under his breath and slumped into a chair as Mrs. Madison came downstairs.

"What happened?" Mrs. Madison asked.

"LeFranco happened. He wouldn't let anyone speak, rushed to vote, and pushed the motion through. Effective immediately."

Mrs. Madison turned pale. "Surely that's not it, then?"

"That's it. It's decided. Marty is looking into legal options, but . . ." Mr. Madison threw up his hands. He looked grimmer than Laurie had ever seen him look.

"What's decided?" Laurie turned off the dog detective show. She wasn't really buying it anyway. She'd never even seen a dog wearing a Sherlock Holmes hat.

Mrs. Madison smoothed Laurie's hair. "Guess you're a Hamilton Hornet now after all, Laurie."

Laurie's stomach dropped. "You mean at the end of the semester? Or the school year?" Leave it to her parents to get all worked up over nothing. It's not like they'd shut the school without any warning.

Mr. Madison gave a scary short laugh. "No, not

at the end of the semester. Now. As soon as they can integrate the students into other schools, they're closing Tuckernuck. Knocking it down to open a stinkin' MegaMart."

Laurie blinked. It couldn't happen that soon, could it? Not when she and Bud were so close to finding the treasure. "But . . . why don't they just wait?"

"Because they don't care about anything but the almighty dollar, that's why. The MegaMart people want the site cleared by the time the ground freezes this winter, and they'll pay big bucks to make sure it happens."

Laurie's mom shot her dad a "time to shut up now" look and pulled Laurie out of her chair. "Think of it this way—you'll be with Kimmy now, right? Why don't you give her a call and let her know?"

Mrs. Madison swatted Laurie on the butt to get her moving, and Laurie headed to her room. She closed her door, but she didn't call Kimmy. For some reason, the sick feeling in the pit of her stomach wouldn't let her.

Bud was working on his word problems when the phone rang. When his mom had died, he and his dad agreed to concentrate on two things—work and each other. And that had worked fine at first. But that was before. Before the whole no-sugar project ruined his life. Before he got a real shot at finding an actual treasure. Now all the extra time spent working on word problems and learning military strategy didn't seem worth it. Bud was pretty sure Laurie's family didn't expect her to make panoramas and do word problems after school, and they probably thought she was plenty well rounded.

"No, I'm sorry, Horace can't come to the phone. He's studying."

Bud heard his dad hang up the phone in the other room.

"Who was that, Dad? Was that for me?" He shoved the word problems away. "Someone was calling me?"

Mr. Wallace came into the living room. "I told her you were studying, Bud."

"But who was it? Can I call them back?" Bud couldn't believe it. Social outcast ever since the whole health food fiasco, and when he *finally* gets a phone call, this is what happens? Not even a stupid message? Bud clenched his fists. "Just for a second, Dad? Please?"

"Remember what we decided? No calls after nine? You can talk to your friend tomorrow. I'm sure whatever it is will keep. Now, how are you doing with these problems?" He picked up Bud's paper.

"Good grief, Dad, I can't even take five minutes for a phone call?" Bud pushed his chair back roughly.

"Bud!" Bud's dad looked shocked. "Where is this coming from? It was just a phone call. Nighttime was going to be Dad and Bud time, remember?"

"I know, but . . ." Bud didn't know what to say. He didn't want to hurt his dad's feelings, but he was so sick of it all. Those stupid rules they'd decided on didn't seem right anymore.

Bud's dad nudged the pencil on the table in line with the paper. "It's not my rule, Bud. We decided these things together," he said quietly.

"Well, maybe we decided wrong, okay? Maybe focusing so much was a bad idea. Mom actually *liked* music and plays and Twinkies and playing around in the yard. Remember? She liked it when I had friends over. Is this really what Mom would've wanted?"

"That's not fair, Bud," Bud's dad said, so softly Bud almost couldn't hear him. He didn't take his eyes off the pencil.

"Well, so what? This isn't fair. None of this."

Bud felt tears stinging the back of his eyes. He snatched the paper away from his dad and tore it up. Then he turned and ran upstairs to his room. Bud was pretty sure he had just officially become the worst person in the world.

Note from Mariah Jeffries to Sam Silver

DID YOU HEAR THE NEWS? I HEARD THEY'RE GOING TO HAVE A WRECKING BALL SMASH THE PLACE ON FRIDAY AFTER THE BELL. CAN YOU BELIEVE IT?
HUGS AND KISSES,
MARIAH

Note from Sam Silver to Mariah Jeffries

Don't make me barf, Mariah.

Note from Hannah Stoller to Calliope Judkin

My dad said that Hamilton has a HUGE food court with fast food from real food places. Hamilton is going to ROCK. And I think Bud Wallace is in the Savannah Heights district, so he won't be able to mess it up.

Note from Calliope Judkin to Bud Wallace

> Did you and Laurie Madison know about this?
> Is that why you've been sneaking around?

Note from Bud Wallace to Calliope Judkin

> I don't know what you're talking about,
> Calliope.

Notes to Bud Wallace and Calliope Judkin

> Mr. Wallace and Miss Judkin:
> I understand we live in exciting times.
> But please refrain from future note passing
> in my class, or I will be forced to send you
> to speak with Principal Winkle.
>   Sincerely,
>   Marshall Deal
>   Sixth-grade science

IMPORTANT MESSAGE

FOR _Principal Winkle_

DATE_____ TIME_____ A.M. P.M.

WHILE YOU WERE OUT

M _Horace Wallace Sr._

OF_____

PHONE NO. _____

TELEPHONED	✓	PLEASE CALL	✓
CALLED TO SEE YOU		WILL CALL AGAIN	
WANTS TO SEE YOU		RUSH	
	RETURNED YOUR CALL		

MESSAGE _Long story short, he wants Bud transferred to Hamilton ASAP. He heard about the school board decision and he worries that the "transitional weeks" will be difficult and will rob his son of his education blah blah blah. Also: I brought a coffee cake from_

SIGNED _Lowell's Bakery. And Olivia made cupcakes. They're in the staff room. Enjoy! Betty_

PRINTED IN U.S.A.

Post-it on Betty's computer

HAVEN'T YOU HEARD
OF FRUIT?
ARE YOU TRYING TO
KILL ME?
                    MARTY

Laurie waited by the front door for Bud, but he wasn't on the bus. Laurie did a scan of the school herself, but she didn't make any real progress. The only thing the stupid school seemed to have were those generic white wall clocks. And unless the word STANDARD was some kind of super-cryptic hint, Laurie wasn't seeing any sign of a clue.

When she spotted Bud just before lunchtime, she made a beeline for him. She didn't know what his problem was, but his attitude was ruining everything.

"What's with you, Bud?" she demanded. "Didn't you hear the news about the school? We barely have any time left before they knock this whole place down."

"I know." Bud shrugged.

"My dad said they'll move us all in the next couple of weeks. But according to Mariah, the wrecking ball's coming Friday. Which means TOMORROW. And Tessa Tysinger says they aren't even waiting until tomorrow, that they're planting plastic explosives as we speak and the school's going to blow after the late bell today. And check it out." Laurie pointed to the far end of the parking lot. "Bulldozers. They're not kidding."

"I know," Bud said again.

"You *know?*" Laurie sputtered. "Then why are you wasting all of our chances to look for clues?"

Bud rolled his eyes. "It's not like I have a choice, okay? My dad picks me up and drops me off now. There's nothing I can do. We'll figure it out at lunch, okay?" His dad hadn't even mentioned their fight when he dropped him off this morning, but Bud knew he was upset. This was not the time to make things worse.

Bud ducked his head down and turned to hurry off, but instead he slammed right into Miss Downey.

"Bud, we missed you at rehearsals. I assume we'll see you from now on?" She gave Bud a penetrating stare that chilled him to the core. Something about that woman was just not right.

"What rehearsals? The school's closing!" Laurie said.

Miss Downey shot her a look that shut Laurie's mouth instantly. "The play has been canceled, and that's sad. But in the meantime, the rest of school life goes on as it always has. Including chorus."

"Uh. Didn't you get the message? About my dad? I can't do that stuff anymore," Bud stammered.

Miss Downey frowned. "And didn't your father get my letter?"

"Yeah, well. Yeah."

Miss Downey's frown got deeper. "I see. Well. We'll see about that." She turned on her heel and went back into the classroom. "Don't leave school today without telling me, Bud," she called over her shoulder.

Bud stared at Laurie wide-eyed. "What the heck is *that* supposed to mean?"

Laurie shrugged. She didn't want to think about Miss Downey and her evil stare of doom. "So we'll search at lunchtime?"

Bud nodded. He hoped this was an easy clue. Because Laurie was right. They were out of time.

"Music hall?"

"Check. Nothing."

"English hall?"

"Check. Nothing."

"Gym?"

"Come on, the gym? Get real." Laurie glared at Bud.

Bud chewed on his pencil. "We have to be thorough. We don't want to miss it."

"Okay, well, check then. Sort of. I mean, I looked, but where would there be a clock? Except for one of those dumb 'standard' ones." Laurie scratched her leg.

Bud nodded. "So what are we missing?"

Laurie shook her head. "Nothing. Except all the places we're not allowed to go. I have the teachers' lounge next on my list, but I don't know how we're going to get into places like storerooms and stuff."

Bud threw his notebook onto the table. "Forget storerooms, I don't know how we're going to get into the teachers' lounge."

Laurie laughed. "That's a piece of cake. Even you could do it."

"Oh, really." Bud wasn't in the mood.

"Sure. All you do is wait until it looks pretty empty, go in, say some teacher is looking for some other teacher, and then scram. That'll get you a look around, at least. If you need more time, ask a question about some assignment."

"Yeah, like that would work."

Laurie got a sly look on her face. "I dare you to try it."

Bud shoved his seat back and marched down the hallway. So what if he got busted, right? They were closing the stinking school.

Laurie hurried after him and watched as he disappeared into the teachers' lounge. He hadn't even stopped to scope the place out first, which in her opinion was a major miscalculation. So she wasn't surprised when he shot back out with a panicked look on his face a few short minutes later.

"So?"

"Mrs. Humphries was taking a nap. Snoring. On a sofa. With . . . with . . ." Bud gulped air and leaned against the wall.

"Spill it. Was there a clock? There had to be a clock." Laurie didn't want to think about Mrs. Humphries taking a nap.

"No clock. But buffalo wings. Dirty napkins all over her stomach and the floor. And orange around her mouth."

Laurie felt her gag reflex kick in, but she fought it back. Mrs. Humphries napping was bad. Buffalo wings were bad. But the two together? She was sorry she'd even dared Bud. That treasure had better be worth all the mental anguish, that's all she had to say.

Laurie positioned herself in front of the door to the student drop-off area and waited until Bud got there to meet his dad. She'd had to barrel out of class at warp speed to beat him there, but she wasn't about to let him get away with ditching the search.

"Seriously?" she said, arms folded. "Seriously? You're really leaving? Without finding the clock? Or whatever it is?"

Bud winced. He knew time was running out, but he wasn't about to let his dad down by not showing up. "It's not like I have a choice. Besides, we don't even know that it is a clock. We could be on the wrong track completely."

Laurie gave Bud a hard stare. Then she relaxed. If he wasn't budging, he wasn't budging. She wasn't going to waste her time on him. "Okay, fine. If you can't, you can't. I'm going to talk to Miss Lucille, see if she knows about any clock that we've missed. Wish me luck."

Laurie patted Bud on the shoulder and headed off down the hall.

"Wait—what?" Bud hesitated and then hurried after her. "You're not going to talk to her without me?"

Laurie didn't even stop. "Why wouldn't I? We're almost out of time, Bud."

Bud hurried after Laurie as she hustled into the main hall. "We've got at least another week, right? In between classes, lunchtime, and there's always gerbil-care time. That will buy us some extra time right there. Ponch and Jon won't mind if we cut their playtime down so we can search."

Laurie pointed violently at the front of the school. "Bulldozers, Bud! What about bulldozers don't you understand?"

Bud winced. "But it's not like they're knocking the school down this second. We've got a little time."

Laurie opened her mouth to respond when a hand came down on her shoulder. Irritated, she shrugged it off and looked up into the face of Mrs. Hutchins.

"Laurie, Bud, just who I was hoping to see!"

Laurie quickly wiped the scowl off her face and slapped on the happy good-student face that she tried to wear when talking to teachers. "Hello, Mrs. Hutchins," she said.

You couldn't really let teachers know when they were butting in at a bad time.

"I wanted to let you know that I'm making a switch in the classroom duty assignments."

"What?" Laurie gasped.

"No!" Bud cried. He'd written that letter a million years ago. She couldn't switch him now.

"Don't worry, you two, I'm keeping you on as Gerbil Monitors. But Calliope here has expressed such an interest in gerbils that I thought she could join you. She's thinking of getting one as a pet."

Calliope sidled up next to Mrs. Hutchins and smirked at them. Laurie hadn't even noticed her lurking back there. "I love the little guys. So cute! And you guys always seem so busy with them, I figured you could use the help."

"What?" Laurie gasped again. She really needed to think of something new to say.

"So starting on Monday, Calliope will join you as Gerbil Monitor Number Three for however long we're here. How does that sound?"

Well, terrible, in a word, but Laurie couldn't really say that. So she put on the big good-student smile again and hoped it would win her brownie points later on. "Super."

"Yeah, great." Bud looked paler than his shirt, and with all the bleach and starch in that thing, that was saying something.

"I wanted to start right away, but Mrs. Hutchins thought Monday would be best." Calliope simpered at them. Her eyes looked cold and hard, though.

"Sounds good to me. Thanks!" Bud grabbed Laurie by the elbow and dragged her away, waving good-bye to Mrs. Hutchins and Calliope.

Note from Calliope Judkin to Secret School Source

I'm in.
Calliope

"Oh, man, Bud." Laurie couldn't believe it. "What are we going to do?" Once Calliope was established as Gerbil Monitor Number Three, gerbil business wouldn't protect them anymore. Calliope would have a reason to interrupt any conversation she came across. They'd never be able to look for treasure safely again.

Bud set his mouth in a grim line. Well, that was that. No more treasure hunting, even if the school survived the weekend. Not with Calliope around all the time.

"Excuse me, kids." A burly guy in a hard hat took Bud by the shoulders and physically moved him out of the way. Then he nodded at them both and headed out the front doors.

"Was that . . ." Laurie stared after the man.

"Yep." Bud hadn't really believed it would happen. But it was happening.

"Did you see any plastic explosives?" Laurie watched as the man disappeared around the corner of the school.

Bud didn't say anything. He felt like throwing up. They weren't kidding. They really were going to destroy the school. And all the clues with it.

Bud set his jaw. He knew he was a huge disappointment. That was pretty obvious. But he wasn't going to be a disappointment as a treasure hunter too.

His dad was going to be upset, Bud knew that. But it would be worth it in the long run. What dad wouldn't be proud of a son who found treasure? It'd be even better than any old speech. Eighth-grade graduation was a million years away anyway.

Bud swallowed hard. "What do we do? We're going to talk to Miss Lucille. We've got to figure this out before Monday."

⁓

"A lamp or clock? Why, yes, I know about a clock." Miss Lucille nodded as she checked in books.

Laurie breathed a sigh of relief. They'd figure this out after all. "Where is it?"

Miss Lucille smiled at her and pointed over her head. "Right there. Isn't it wonderful? They have one in every classroom now."

Laurie ignored the groaning noise coming behind her. Bud could use some lessons in tact. "Yes, I know about those wall clocks. And they sure are great. . . ."

Miss Lucille nodded in appreciation. Apparently to her, those wall clocks were the best things since sliced bread.

"But is there another clock around? Maybe a desk clock or a different wall clock? One that was here when Maria Tutweiler opened the school? One that"—she sniffled dramatically—"Mrs. Reynolds may have used?" It was a cheap ploy, but she didn't know how to get through to Miss Lucille otherwise.

Miss Lucille's face immediately crumpled up in sympathy. "Oh, you poor dear." She stopped checking in books and patted Laurie's hand. "There were clocks, yes, beautiful clocks, some big, some small, all different kinds. Mrs. Tutweiler had a big, beautiful one right in the front hall. But then we got these wonderful wall clocks and we didn't need them anymore." She patted Laurie's hand again. "Believe me, dear, Mrs. Reynolds would've loved the wall clocks."

Laurie nodded. "I bet she would've."

"Thanks, Miss Lucille," Bud said, pulling Laurie's hand away from Miss Lucille's patting hand. It was starting to turn pink under all the patting and rubbing.

Laurie looked back as she headed out of the library in time to see Miss Lucille point at the wall clock and give her a big thumbs-up.

Bud sighed. "Face it, Laurie. If the clock was in the school, it's gone now. And I don't know how we're going to track it down."

Laurie stopped walking and leaned against a locker.

"So that's it, then." She scanned the hallway as if she expected the clue clock to magically appear and dance a jig in front of the lockers.

"Where the heck would fifty-year-old office equipment go?" Bud said. If there was a way to track it down, he would. But he didn't even know where to start. "Look on the bright side. If it's not in the school anymore, the school getting demolished doesn't matter. We have lots of time."

Laurie nodded, but she didn't look at him. "Maybe we can just skip that clue? Start looking for weird inscriptions or big letters? Maybe we don't need to find that clue to find the one that comes after it."

Bud shifted his book bag onto his other shoulder. "Yeah, we'll do that. That's a good idea," Bud lied. It would be like looking for a needle in a haystack. Still, he guessed there was a chance it could work.

"We won't know what letter we're missing though. Or even if we've found the right next clue. It's going to mess up the whole 'I HAD' part of the clue."

"Yeah, well . . ." Bud couldn't stand to see Laurie looking so gloomy. "How stupid was it to use things that move to hide clues? Way to go, Tutweiler," he said sarcastically.

Laurie didn't say anything. She just stared over Bud's shoulder with a weird expression on her face.

"I mean, like the clues were so simple and easy to find, right? Good grief," Bud went on. But Laurie didn't seem to be listening at all.

"Bud, what does your dad look like?" Laurie whispered.

Bud went cold. He'd gotten so wrapped up in how proud his dad would be about the treasure that he'd kind of glossed over how ticked off his dad was going to be when he didn't show up in the parking lot. He didn't need to turn around and look to know what he would see. And sure enough, his dad was storming up the hallway, frowning so hard it was surprising he could even see where he was going. Principal Winkle was hurrying along behind him with a panicked look on his face.

Bud's throat went dry. "Uh, hi, Dad."

"Bud, I told you to come see me before you left. Is this your father?" Miss Downey appeared from the music hall and stood next to him, watching his dad approach.

Bud just nodded.

"Good. I need to speak with you both." Miss Downey took Bud by the shoulder and went up to Bud's dad. "Mr. Wallace, thank you for coming. Principal Winkle? We'll be using your office now."

"Of course, of course." Principal Winkle looked as confused as Bud felt. Even Mr. Wallace seemed thrown by Miss Downey.

Laurie followed the group as they went into Principal Winkle's office and closed the door.

Then she settled down next to the lockers and started

on her homework. There was no way she was missing the fireworks when that door opened again.

⌇

Laurie had already finished her math homework and started on her science before the door to Principal Winkle's office opened and Bud staggered out.

He looked awful—pale and with an expression she'd only seen once before, when Trip Ailiff had gotten hit in the head with the dodgeball three times in one period. It wasn't a good look.

"What happened?" she asked, scrambling to her feet. "What did they do to you?"

Bud opened his mouth to answer, but before he could, the door to Principal Winkle's office opened again. Laurie and Bud watched as Miss Downey and Mr. Wallace came out into the hall.

Laughing. And smiling. Miss Downey had her hand on Mr. Wallace's arm. It was the weirdest thing Laurie'd ever seen in her life.

"Okay then, Wally, we have a deal. Bye-bye!" Miss Downey called to Bud's dad as she turned to go back to her classroom. Horace Wallace Sr.'s ears turned pink.

Laurie's jaw dropped and she stared at Bud in disbelief.

Bud gave her a wide-eyed shrug.

Principal Winkle came out of his office and started talking with Mr. Wallace, so Laurie grabbed Bud and dragged him a few feet away.

"Okay, they can't hear us. What happened in there?"

"I've never seen anything like it. It's like she's a witch, Laurie, an honest-to-god witch with spells and magical powers and everything. Spells. But listen, okay? Listen."

Bud reached out, grabbed Laurie's arms, and stared at her intently. He was freaking her out. It was pretty obvious he'd gone insane. Scary eyes insane. Miss Downey was the least witch-like person Laurie had ever seen. Witches don't wear dresses with tiny flowers on them. Witches don't kick the juice machine when it malfunctions. Witches don't talk about buying stuff on QVC. They just don't.

"Laurie, listen," Bud said again. "Forget about that. That doesn't matter, okay?"

Laurie nodded her appease-the-crazy-person nod. "Okay, Bud. What matters?"

Bud's face broke out into a huge smile. "I found the clock."

EVIDENCE THAT MISS DOWNEY IS A WITCH

by Bud Wallace (as requested by Laurie Madison)

1. Able to cast spells.

    PROOF: Dad is downstairs singing. Seriously. A real song and everything.

2. Spell casting.

    PROOF: Dad, whistling on the drive home.

3. Spells.

    PROOF: Dad encouraged me to take up piano again and "take chorus seriously."

4. Mind reading.

    PROOF: Knew instantly that me and Dad were trying to avoid hurting each other's feelings. How else could she know that?

5. Bewitching people (with spells).

    PROOF: Dad asked which tie looks more fashionable, the blue one or the red one. Fashionable? They're ties.

CONCLUSION: She's a witch.

Addendum
added by Laurie Madison, skeptical nonbeliever, grade six

Pretty thin evidence, Bud.

CONCLUSION: Not proven.

PART SEVEN

OPERATION WINKLE

WAYS INTO PRINCIPAL WINKLE'S OFFICE
by Laurie Madison, grade six

1. Break in.

   PROS: We get the goods.

   CONS: Could get caught, life of crime, etc.

2. Figure out way to get sent to office.

   PROS: We're in.

   CONS: Bad for permanent record, plus Winkle would be there. Can't hunt for clue with him there.

3. Get Winkle to take clock out.

   PROS: He does all the work for us.

   CONS: No idea how to do that.

4. Lure Winkle out.

   PROS: Empty office just waiting.

   CONS: Need to find weakness. Cookies?

"We're never getting in there," Bud said from his watch point outside Principal Winkle's office. "Security in that office is tighter than a fortress. Even if we could get inside, he never leaves. What's up with that?"

Laurie nodded in agreement. "It's like he's not even human. Did I tell you how long I spent on those whole-wheat bars? And he didn't touch one!"

Laurie had come up with the bright idea of baking chocolate chip cookies and putting them out on the common area table. But since cookies were still on the school's official banned junk food list, she'd had to go with her backup—whole-wheat raisin bars. Principal Winkle hadn't even taken one, not even when Laurie had used her tiny battery-operated fan to make the fumes of wheaty goodness waft into his office. He'd just taken an apple out of a bowl on his desk and closed the door.

"More gerbil business, you two? Maybe you better fill me in." Calliope Judkin squatted down next to them. Laurie started. Seriously, if anyone was in the running for the witch label, it was Calliope. She'd been popping up out of nowhere lately.

"Nothing to worry about," Bud said gruffly. Calliope was going to be a problem. He was going to have to come up with a way to let her down gently.

"Well, as Gerbil Monitor Number Three, I need to know." Calliope smiled.

"We'll fill you in on official gerbil business on Monday," Laurie said, scowling.

Calliope smiled again. "You better, or Mrs. Hutchins might dock your grade." She sauntered away, looking very pleased with herself.

Bud rolled his eyes at Laurie. "Well, Monday's sure going to stink," he said.

Laurie gave him an evil grin. "Maybe. But today is going to be awesome. Come on, we've got important gerbil business."

~

Ponch and Jon were enthusiastic about their part in the mission. At least Laurie thought they were. She'd told them about it, but since they were rodents there was a good chance they didn't quite understand their role. But they definitely knew something was up and were raring to go.

Laurie went over her checklist one last time.

"Okay, reconnaissance. You're sure we're good there?" That was the thing Laurie was most concerned about. Ponch and Jon were essential to the plan, but there was no way she was going ahead with it if they might get hurt somehow.

"Check." Bud had personally scoped out the area around Principal Winkle's office between classes. No niches or crevices, and no rogue exit routes that would endanger the tiny fighting duo. If Bud calculated correctly, it was pretty much a straight shot, in and out, no complications. The big risk was if Principal Winkle

took a moment to realize how unlikely the whole scenario was. But given the way things went at this school,
Bud didn't think that was going to be an issue.

Laurie grabbed Ponch (or Jon) and Bud grabbed
Jon (or Ponch) and they headed out into the hallway,
nervously checking the emptying hallways. They'd
decided to go for maximum impact with a minimum of
witnesses. And that meant putting the plan into motion
between the final bell and the late bell.

"Is he in there?" Laurie peered around the corner at
Principal Winkle's office.

"He's in there," Bud said.

"Then let's go." Laurie could tell Ponch (or Jon) was
getting pretty impatient and wanted to get the show on
the road. Besides, her hand was starting to sweat, and
his fur was getting matted and clumpy. Not a good look
for a gerbil.

"Now!" Bud rushed forward with Jon (or Ponch) and
ducked down beside Principal Winkle's office. Laurie
did the same thing on the other side of the door. And
then, simultaneously, they opened their fists.

Ponch and Jon couldn't believe their good luck. Not
only were they out of the cage, they were in an exciting
new locale that smelled like a tantalizing mixture of fruit

and chocolate. This was obviously the place to be. They couldn't believe they'd never checked it out before.

Without hesitating, both of the gerbils rushed into Principal Winkle's office.

"Wait for it," Bud whispered. They had to give the gerbils enough time, or the whole thing would be for nothing. He knew he could count on those two to work fast, though.

It took even less time than he thought.

"What the—*whaAAAAAhhh!*" If Principal Winkle's scream had been any higher, only dogs would've been able to hear it. As it was, Laurie and Bud recognized their cue and sprang into action.

"Ponch? Jon? Where are you? Oh, no!" Laurie rushed into Principal Winkle's office, doing her best to look panicky and out of breath.

Bud slammed into her from behind, totally knocking the wind out of her and making them look like bumbling incompetents. Laurie felt like high-fiving him. It was just the impression they were going for.

"Did two gerbils come in here, Principal Winkle?" Laurie said, pretending to scan the room. Like she couldn't see Ponch (or Jon) totally scarfing down a cupcake wrapper that had missed the trash can by a couple of inches. The trash can right next to the ancient-looking carved clock.

"I . . . I believe . . . there are . . . they . . . YES!" Principal Winkle looked freaked out and ready to jump onto his chair. Which would've been pretty funny, but it wasn't what they were going for.

"They got loose again," Laurie said apologetically. "We couldn't stop them."

"Maybe you could go outside?" Bud said, watching Jon (or Ponch) quietly sidling up to Principal Winkle's foot. Principal Winkle didn't seem to be aware of him yet. "We'll catch them."

Principal Winkle nodded. "That's good, kids, catch them. Just close the door, why don't you? That way they can't get out."

Laurie suppressed a grin. This was going just the way they'd hoped. She and Bud waited expectantly for Principal Winkle to leave. But he just kept standing in a half crouch behind his desk.

Finally Bud cleared his throat. "So are you . . . uh . . . going into the hall now?"

Principal Winkle waved his hand at Bud. "Just close the door, I'll be fine. We don't want them to . . . *aaaahh!*" Principal Winkle made the leap from floor to desk chair as he noticed Jon (or Ponch) doing a taste test on his shoe leather.

Laurie gritted her teeth. She was so close to the clock she could've grabbed it and stuffed it under her shirt. Except (a) it was a grandfather clock and way too big to fit under a shirt, and (b) Winkle would totally see her do it. It was time for a new plan.

"There's one!" Laurie said, suddenly pretending to notice Ponch (or Jon) and his half-eaten cupcake wrapper. She made a clumsy dive for the surprised rodent, who gave her a panicked glare (since lunging was not in the plan she'd described to him earlier) and tried to decide whether to feint to the right or to the left or just go for the jugular.

"Shoot, missed him," Laurie said loudly, hoping nobody noticed the angry and freaked out rodent that she'd scooped up and who was currently having a hissy fit in her fist. "What's that one doing?" she asked, pointing at Jon (or Ponch), who was currently wondering why Principal Winkle had shot upward so quickly, taking his tasty footwear with him.

Then, when both Bud and Principal Winkle were distracted and looking at the floor, she chucked Ponch (or Jon) onto the desk. "Wow, did you see that jump?" Laurie gasped.

Principal Winkle looked up. "What jum—*aiiieee!*"

Ponch (or Jon) was definitely working his heart out. Finding himself suddenly on Principal Winkle's day planner, he did what any normal red-blooded gerbil would do. After doing a quick surveillance scan, he (a) relieved himself, (b) made his scariest face at Principal Winkle, and (c) attacked a nearby Milky Way bar.

Principal Winkle screamed again and leaped for the door. "I'll be outside I have an important—just catch them!"

He dragged the door shut behind him.

Laurie and Bud didn't waste any time. "Get the clock!" Laurie said, gracefully scooping up Ponch (or Jon) with one hand without disturbing his day-planner leavings.

Bud gave the clock a quick once-over. It was an ornately carved grandfather-type clock, tall, with dark wood and, most importantly, a long door on the front. Bud hoped the clue was in there, because there was nothing obvious carved on the paneling or on the face of the clock. No saying, no letters, nothing.

He grabbed the tiny latch and opened the door just as Laurie scooped up a squirmy Jon (or Ponch) from where he'd just discovered the uneaten remains of the cupcake wrapper.

"Is it in there?" she whispered.

Bud scanned the inside of the clock. There was a shallow shelf that was empty except for the clock's winding key, and that was it. Bud felt like he was going to throw up. This couldn't all be for nothing.

"Nothing?" Laurie gasped. "Are you kidding?"

Bud couldn't say anything. There had to be something. He squatted down to inspect the inside of the clock, looking for some sign of a fake wall or a secret door. And that's when he noticed the envelope.

"There it is! It has to be!" From above, the envelope was completely hidden, but from his position on the floor, Bud could see an ancient-looking manila envelope carefully taped under the shallow shelf.

"Get it!" Laurie hissed, watching the door. "Hurry up!"

Bud grabbed the envelope and stuffed it into the waistband in the back of his pants just as the door opened a crack.

Principal Winkle peeked in. "All good?" he said. He sounded like he'd just realized how embarrassing it was to be chased out of his office by two tiny classroom pets.

"All good," Laurie said, blocking Bud from view as he closed the clock door. "We got 'em." She held up Ponch and Jon. "Sorry about that."

Principal Winkle sighed and opened the door fully.

"Good, good. Now don't let those two escape like that again. They could get hurt. I don't want to see them back in here."

He looked around nervously, like he was afraid Ponch and Jon had given off baby-gerbil spores in the few moments they'd spent in his office.

"Don't worry." Bud grinned. "You won't see us back in here."

EMAIL
FROM: PRINCIPAL MARTIN WINKLE, Tuckernuck Hall
TO: OLIVIA HUTCHINS
SUBJECT: Surprise Visit

Olivia,

I saw your furry classroom friends today, and they seemed remarkably fit and healthy. Quite the jumpers, aren't they? Do you think they might have outgrown their cage, though? Do you need a larger, more secure area for them, perhaps? Just want to keep the little guys happy and, most importantly, secure.

Thanks,

Marty

EMAIL

FROM: OLIVIA HUTCHINS:

TO: PRINCIPAL MARTIN WINKLE, Tuckernuck Hall

SUBJECT: Two Very Happy Gerbils!

Marty—

I didn't realize you had stopped by! Ponch and Jon would love that. They are very active and would enjoy more space to play. I've attached a link to the Deluxe Gerbil Playhouse in the latest Rodent Paradise catalog.

Thanks for thinking of us!

Olivia

Once Laurie and Bud had returned the exhausted and well-fed gerbil friends to their cage, they turned to the envelope.

Bud pulled the slightly crumpled envelope from the waistband of his pants and looked at Laurie for a second. "You realize Principal Winkle had candy in his office, don't you? That's got to be a violation of some kind."

Laurie rolled her eyes at him. "We'll deal with that later. Now open the stinking envelope!"

Bud smiled and slowly untwined the long, looping

string holding the envelope flap down. Laurie sighed. He was really milking it for all it was worth.

Finally the flap came loose, and Bud slid the papers out onto the desk. It was a letter, and with it came an elaborate paper cutout letter L.

"It looks like a doily," Laurie said, her fingers hovering near the intricate edges of the L.

"And it's an L," Bud nodded. So that means . . ."

"That means we still have more clues to find. Because I HAD L doesn't make any sense." Laurie didn't want to waste any time.

"Right. So let's see what she says." There was no mistaking Maria Tutweiler's spidery handwriting. They'd both pored over the first note so many times they could practically see it in their sleep.

> *CONGRATULATIONS, BRAVE ADVENTURERS!*
>
> *You have done well and come far. Everything you need to solve the puzzle is in your grasp, as it has been since you set out on your journey. But if you need a final nudge, here is one final clue.*
>
> *See you at the finish line!*
>
> *Maria Tutweiler*

If you enter the school from the rear entrance, pass that which makes the blood flow, turn left to pass the wisdom of the ages, and turn right as you reach that which stirs our souls. When you reach the heart of the mind, fifty paces to your left shall lead you to your journey's end.

Bud looked at Laurie and shrugged. "Yeah, beats me."

At the front of the school, a loud rumbling noise started up. A noise like bulldozers starting.

Bud bit his lip. "Probably just moving them, right?"

Laurie nodded. They'd better be.

"Race you to the back entrance?" Bud got in a runner pose.

"You bet," Laurie said, taking off down the hall. She had no idea what Maria Tutweiler was talking about, but they'd figure it out. They had to.

PART EIGHT

MARIA TUTWEILER'S TREASURE

"Okay, here goes nothing." Bud took a deep breath, and he and Laurie stepped into the back entrance to the school simultaneously.

"Do you see it?" Laurie whispered. They were taking super-slow baby steps, like they expected an ambush or a trapdoor to open at any moment.

"See what?" Bud whispered back.

"That which makes our blood flow."

"Nope," Bud said, a chill running down his back. Blood flowing sure didn't sound good. He hadn't really planned on any physical confrontations in this whole hunting-for-treasure thing, and he wasn't really excited about starting now. He wished he'd brought some kind of weapon. Anything. Even the beef stick he'd eaten before school would've made him feel better.

"That which makes our blood flow," Laurie whispered again. They were passing locker after locker. Nothing really bloody about lockers.

Just past the lockers, Laurie stopped abruptly. "Is that it?" She blinked at Bud.

"What?" He looked around, but he wasn't seeing anything unusual. "What are you looking at?"

"Not looking, listen." Laurie's ears were almost pricking up, she was concentrating so hard. "The gym.

Isn't that what people say? That exercise gets your blood moving?"

"Makes the blood flow . . . ," Bud said thoughtfully. "I bet that's it." He looked at the clue again. "Okay, so now we just go on past to the wisdom of ages. Then we hang a left."

Laurie shrugged. "Oh, is that all? No problem." She snickered. "I've got a good feeling about this one."

They walked on, past the gym, past more lockers, and then suddenly Laurie jogged on ahead.

She gave a little cheer and turned back. "I knew it! The library! Wisdom of ages for sure!"

Bud grinned. This was going to be a cinch. "Hang a left!"

They headed to the left, waved to Miss Lucille, and hurried up the hallway toward the English hall.

"Okay, hold up, what's next?" Laurie stretched out her arm to stop Bud in his tracks.

He looked down at the paper. "That which stirs our souls?" He frowned. "Maybe. It could be that one."

Laurie started into the English hall. "Was this always the English hall, though? I mean, the library was always the library, and the gym was always the gym, but the classrooms?"

She shook her head. "I don't know."

Bud looked around. "Well, I do. No place to make a right here anyway. So we keep going."

They continued on, a little more slowly than before. They rejected the music hall and the science hall (no right turns there either) and finally came to Reynolds Auditorium.

Bud grinned at Laurie. "That which stirs our souls?"

Laurie held up her hand for a high five. "Oh, yeah, definitely. This is awesome." Bud didn't connect in his attempt to high five, but the thought was there, and that's what counts.

They made a right. "You know, I'm glad this isn't like the other clues. This is pretty much a gimme," Laurie said, jogging along scanning the hallways.

"It's like a victory lap," Bud said. "Check it out." He pointed ahead. "How much do you want to bet we're at 'the heart of the mind.'"

Laurie looked up to see the administrative offices in front of them.

"Trust the school founder to think of her office as 'the heart of the mind.'" Bud chuckled.

Laurie could hardly believe they were so close to finding the treasure. She didn't really think it was gold bars anymore, but it might be a chest of jewels. That was a definite possibility. And it would be all hers. Well, hers and Bud's, whatever.

In front of the office door they came to a screeching halt. Bud looked serious and consulted the clue again. "Okay, this is where we have to be careful. Fifty paces to the left. So I guess regular-size steps?"

Laurie nodded. "Not too big, okay? Just normal."

Counting under their breath, Laurie and Bud carefully made their way step by step down the hall. Hannah Stoller passed them on the way to her locker, but they didn't even notice the weird look she gave them. They were so close.

"Forty-eight, forty-nine, fifty." Bud and Laurie stopped and looked around, practically holding their breath in anticipation.

"And . . . what the heck?" Bud's shoulders slumped. "Huh?" He looked at the clue carefully. "Maybe we did it wrong?"

Laurie shrugged. Their fifty careful steps had led them right back to the front hall of the school. Right back to the big empty area with the ugly paintings of people and things named everything but Hope. "This makes no sense."

"Should we try again?" Bud said, a desperate look in his eyes.

The bulldozers had moved closer to the school—so close that they could see one of the construction guys spit into the grass.

Laurie sighed. "We'd better."

EMAIL

FROM: MARSHALL DEAL, Tuckernuck Hall

TO: FLORA DOWNEY, Tuckernuck Hall

SUBJECT: What was that?

Flora:

Are you still working on that play? I saw two of your students doing what I can only assume was rehearsing in the hallway this afternoon.

I thought Winkle said those activities were cancelled?

Marshall

EMAIL

FROM: FLORA DOWNEY, Tuckernuck Hall

TO: MARSHALL DEAL, Tuckernuck Hall

RE: What was what?

Students of mine? No students of mine were rehearsing today. What were they doing?

EMAIL
FROM: MARSHALL DEAL, Tuckernuck Hall
TO: FLORA DOWNEY, Tuckernuck Hall
SUBJECT: Never Mind

Never mind then. I bet it's some new craze. Something they saw on the internet. You know how kids are.

After three more tries led them right back to the front hall, Laurie and Bud gave up. They slumped down underneath the portrait of Hilda the ratty-looking chicken and spread out all the clues and letters in front of them. Laurie had done a pretty admirable job of making cutout versions of the H and A letters and had been keeping them in her locker with the others. Bud picked up the A and glared at it.

"I don't even care who sees," Bud said defiantly, looking around at the empty hallway like he was daring the invisible people to look at Maria Tutweiler's papers. "We messed up somewhere."

Laurie just sighed. "Maybe we should look at the letters again? That might help."

"What, I HAD L? That's going to help? How's that going to help, Laurie?" Bud couldn't believe it. His dad was right. All of this had just been a big waste of time. He would've been better off studying.

Laurie didn't say anything; she just fiddled with the wooden D. Finally she looked up. "Okay, how about this. What if it isn't I HAD L? What if it's . . ." She took the A from Bud and rearranged the letters with a dramatic flourish. "LAD HI?"

Bud gave a short barky laugh. "Lad hi? What the heck's that supposed to mean? Wouldn't HI LAD make more sense?"

Laurie shrugged.

"So what, Tutweiler's just saying howdy? That's the treasure, a friendly greeting? That's really dumb, Laurie."

Laurie watched Bud's face as he ranted. It was actually kind of interesting the way it was changing from pink to white and back again in random blotches across his face. She wondered what was going to happen next. If she had to bet, she would go with foaming at the mouth.

"Or why stop at HI LAD?" Bud said, obviously on a

roll. "Why not make it IL HAD? Or HA LID? Or HIL DA?" Bud's voice died away as he looked at the word he'd just spelled out. All of the blotchy pink drained away from his face.

"Hilda?" Laurie and Bud looked at each other and then immediately craned their necks to look at the painting over their heads. The scrawny chicken in the portrait gazed back at them with a smug look in its eye.

~~

"That is just sick." Bud said. They'd been staring at the portrait for what felt like a million years. "I can't believe we fell for a joke by some twisted, chicken-obsessed freak. Wow, that's pathetic."

Laurie had to agree. If the treasure was all a big joke, she would've appreciated someone filling her in before she'd spent the first three weeks of school—the most important time for forming social bonds—hanging out with the class outcast. Nobody had ever suggested that the big treasure might end up being a lame chicken portrait.

"Maybe you were supposed to tell Tutweiler when you'd figured it out? And then she'd hand you the treasure?" Laurie said doubtfully.

"Yeah, well, fat lot of good that does us now," Bud

said bitterly. "It's really just mean. And it's not even a good chicken. If you're going for a gag prize, why not go all the way and make the treasure 'Dogs Playing Poker' or a velvet Elvis?" Bud was so mad at Maria Tutweiler he wanted to spit.

"Well, whatever. It's not like she didn't warn us," Laurie said finally, adjusting her book bag. She wasn't even going to tell Jack she'd actually found the treasure. He'd just laugh his butt off when he heard what it was, and she really didn't need that right now.

"What do you mean?" Bud said.

"Oh, you know . . ." Laurie held out her hand and waggled her fingers impatiently. "Give me the first one—that first clue? What did it say?"

Bud handed her the first note from Maria Tutweiler.

Laurie scanned the clue for a second. "See? Listen to this. *'Now it is time for you to make a choice. You can continue on and follow my clues wherever they may lead, or you may remain here, where you started.'"* Laurie gave Bud a significant look. "She basically told us right there that there was no point and we were going to end up right where we started. We were just too dumb to figure it out."

They stared at the painting again for a second.

"Unless . . . ," Bud said tentatively. He glanced at Laurie.

"What?" Bud had a really weird look on his face that Laurie wasn't getting.

"Remember the back of that painting? Where the clue was?" Bud raised his eyebrows at her.

"Sure. There was that hole back there. And a rip . . . ," Laurie said slowly. One corner of her mouth quirked up. "Oh, man . . ."

It was like someone had shot off a starter pistol, they raced for the painting so fast. They didn't even bother to check to make sure the coast was clear before they lunged for it. Bud grabbed the side of the frame and tried to wrestle it to the ground, while Laurie lifted from the bottom, hoping to unhook it from the wall. A little manhandling later, the painting came loose, almost squashing Laurie underneath, but somehow they managed to keep it from smashing onto the floor.

"Anything?" Laurie gasped, struggling under the weight of the picture. The top of the frame was digging into her collarbone painfully.

"There's definitely something . . . ," Bud said, trying to maneuver around to see the bottom of the frame. His fingers were turning white from gripping the edge.

"I can definitely see—"

But as close as she was, Laurie missed the rest of Bud's sentence. Because no matter how close you are, it's hard to hear when piercing shrieks are echoing off the walls.

IMPORTANT MESSAGE

FOR *Police Chief Skip Burkiss*

DATE_____ TIME_____ A.M. / P.M.

WHILE YOU WERE OUT

M *Betty Abernathy*

OF_____

PHONE NO. _____

TELEPHONED		PLEASE CALL	
CALLED TO SEE YOU		WILL CALL AGAIN	
WANTS TO SEE YOU	✓	RUSH	✓
RETURNED YOUR CALL			

MESSAGE *Skip, Betty Abernathy down at Tuckernuck Hall called—something about a theft or disturbance? She needs you to come out ASAP. Something about chickens, she was screaming too much and wasn't being clear.*

SIGNED *Also, don't forget I'm taking a half day tomorrow. Luralene*

PRINTED IN U.S.A.

Bud and Laurie sat in Principal Winkle's office, staring at his empty desk. They could tell by the way everyone was whispering that they were in big trouble.

"I don't know which is worse," Betty Abernathy hissed at them as she marched in and deposited a file on Principal Winkle's desk. "The thought that you were trying to steal the painting, or that you were just destroying it for your own malicious pleasure."

"We weren't doing ei—" Laurie started.

"Hsst!" Betty Abernathy spit the word and glared. "Not a word! Not a word out of you until your parents arrive!" Then she stalked back out of the room without a backward glance.

Laurie nudged Bud. "I can't believe they won't even let us explain," she whispered. "At least they sent Calliope home. It would stink if she were here gloating."

Bud shrugged and gave a rueful smile. He didn't really understand what anybody was saying. Calliope Judkin had seen them through the office window and started screaming, and then rushed up and latched on to Bud until Miss Abernathy and Principal Winkle ran out. That girl had some vocal cords. His ears were still ringing.

He didn't really care what anyone said, though. They

knew where the treasure was. And once they spilled those beans, nothing else would matter.

"Since Betty took it upon herself to alert the authorities, I thought it best that the children have parental representation for our talk," Principal Winkle explained. Flanking him on the right and the left were Betty Abernathy, who looked like she wanted to grind Bud and Laurie up and feed them to the pigs, and Mrs. Hutchins, who looked pretty surprised.

Laurie slumped down in her chair. Her dad didn't seem mad, exactly, just a little confused. She and Bud hadn't had time to fill their parents in on anything. Bud's dad looked like he was going to freak out.

"So you believe our children were trying to steal from the school?" Mr. Wallace said. His voice sounded too loud in the little room. "You expect us to believe they were trying to steal *that*?"

He pointed to the Hilda portrait, which was now leaning up against Principal Winkle's wall.

"They were caught either stealing or destroying it."

"Well, it would certainly match our decor, right, Bud?" Mr. Wallace gave a nervous laugh. Laurie wished he'd shut his mouth so they could explain. He really wasn't helping.

"We weren't—" she started.

"You don't have to say anything, Laurie," her dad said. He had worry lines around his eyes.

"No, it's okay, because . . . ," she started, but Bud cut her off.

"We found the treasure," Bud said nonchalantly.

Laurie glared at him. Trust Bud to steal her thunder.

"Yeah, we did. The two of us." Laurie felt a little better once she'd staked her claim.

"I see," Principal Winkle said carefully. Destructive children were one thing, but mentally unbalanced children meant he was definitely missing his dinner reservation, and maybe even the movie afterward too. "The treasure?"

"Come on!" Laurie rolled her eyes. "Maria Tutweiler's treasure? We found it, okay? It's right there."

She pointed to the painting of Hilda, which was looking more mangy and disreputable than ever.

"She's right," Bud said, smirking.

"Well, that's wonderful. Congratulations." Principal Winkle looked significantly at the two dads. "If I might speak with the two of you"—he nodded his head—"outside."

"No!" Laurie sat up. "Look, we found the first clue. And we solved it, right? And then that led us to the cat, except it was dead."

"Dead cat. I see." Principal Winkle wished he'd taken that child psych course over the summer. He looked at Olivia Hutchins, who shrugged helplessly. They'd seemed like two normal kids when school started.

"Show them, Bud. Show them the clues," Laurie barked.

Bud slowly sat up, opened his notebook, and tossed the papers onto the desk. Then he sat back cockily and grinned.

"I don't see how that—" Principal Winkle started, but Olivia Hutchins suddenly leaned forward.

"That's her handwriting, Marty. Maria Tutweiler, that's her writing." Her eyes were wide.

"What? Really?" He examined the papers with their spidery handwriting and picked up the lacy letter L.

Mrs. Hutchins picked up the final clue and read it, her hand trembling. "Where did you get these?"

Bud opened his mouth to answer, but Principal Winkle held up his hand to silence him. He stared at Laurie and Bud for a moment. "You found the treasure?"

Laurie and Bud both nodded.

Principal Winkle picked up the telephone. "I'm calling our lawyers. And then you two better start at the beginning."

———✐———

Banner on the Morning News *website*

BREAKING NEWS!
TUTWEILER TREASURE FOUND!
"It's not a myth after all," say sources.

Full story in the *Morning News*!

———✐———

"I can't believe we're doing this," Mrs. Hutchins said, holding the matte knife between two fingers. "We're really going to cut into the back of this painting? It's an antique."

"I checked with legal. We've got witnesses, we've got probable cause, we're covered."

"Yes, but . . ."

"Take a look at it, Olivia. It's a chicken." Principal Winkle hefted the painting onto his desk.

"Yes, but . . ."

"It's not just a chicken. It's a hideous chicken. If Tutweiler hadn't put it in the school charter, I would've gotten rid of it years ago." Principal Winkle had never been a big fan of bad art.

Bud and Laurie exchanged glances. "What do you mean, put it in the charter?" Laurie said, taking the knife from Mrs. Hutchins.

"There were certain items that had to remain in the school. It was known as the Tutweiler rule. This painting is one of them."

Bud groaned. "Let me guess. The bust of Homer is another one?"

"And that clock?" Laurie said. "That didn't tip you off?"

Principal Winkle sighed. "Apparently I wasn't as observant as I could've been. Anything unusual was chalked up to Tutweiler eccentricity. Now are we going to do this?"

He looked at the matte knife in Laurie's hand expectantly.

"Go to it, kids," Laurie's dad said quietly. The dads had been relegated to the corner of the office with instructions to be quiet and stay out of the way. But it was harder than it looked.

"Actually, we may not need that," Bud said, reaching out and picking tentatively at the rip in the paper. "I think it's just here."

Slowly Bud tore back the brittle brown paper. But it wasn't the back of the Hilda portrait they found behind the paper. It was another large manila envelope fastened to a stiff piece of cardboard.

"It's got a false back," Principal Winkle breathed. "All this time, it's had a false back."

"Well, thank goodness we didn't have to hurt Hilda," Mrs. Hutchins said. "I like her."

Mr. Wallace opened his mouth to say something, but after Mrs. Hutchins fixed him with a glare, he wisely shut it again.

Bud pulled out the manila envelope and handed it to Laurie, who slowly undid the string fastener. Then she pulled out a large sheaf of papers.

Mrs. Hutchins immediately pounced on the bundle of boring-looking records while Laurie read Maria Tutweiler's last note aloud.

AT LONG LAST THE TREASURE IS YOURS. CONGRATULATIONS! You have demonstrated the qualities of a true Tuckernuck Clucker—diligence, intelligence, good humor, and excellent problem-solving skills. I am happy to present you with the official

> *Tuckernuck Spirit Stick, which you will find under Hilda's careful guard.*

Principal Winkle pulled back a bit more of the brown paper backing. "Ah. Here we go," he said, pulling out an elaborately carved wooden stick. He handed it to Bud.

"A stick?" Bud stared at it in disbelief. The treasure was a Spirit Stick? Sure, it was nice for a stick, but it was still just . . . a stick. "That's it?"

Laurie growled deep in the back of her throat. If she'd gone though all this just for a stick . . . "It better not be. Let me finish," Laurie went back to the letter.

> *The Tuckernuck Spirit Stick carries with it great responsibilities. For these few months . . .*

"Try years," Bud said.

"Try decades," Principal Winkle said.

"Shh!" Mrs. Hutchins and Laurie both hissed.

> *months, you have labored under the undignified moniker of Tuckernuck Clucker. As the first*

bearer of the Tuckernuck Spirit Stick, I give you and only you the power to change your school's identity, if you truly feel it is an undue burden on your classmates. Though I enjoy the lighthearted moniker, I will abide by your decision.

"Wow, for real?" Laurie dropped the paper down and gaped at the others.

"You're not going to do it, are you?" Principal Winkle said, trying not to look at his Clucker hat hanging on the wall. He was more than a little attached.

"Of course not! We won't let them!" Miss Abernathy said huffily.

"According to that, it's up to them," Principal Winkle said.

"We'll decide later," Bud said. He secretly liked being a Clucker. He figured all he had to do was think up a new name so terrible that Laurie would decide she wanted to stay a Clucker too. "Go on."

Laurie nodded and went back to the letter.

As the bearers of the Spirit Stick, it is up to you to continue this fine Tuckernuck tradition in the coming years. So it will be up to you to create next year's Treasure Hunt, to challenge and engage your fellow students.

"Oh, man, that rocks," Bud said.

Laurie nodded in agreement. She already had a ton of good hiding places in mind. Places that didn't have anything to do with dead cats. She went back to the note.

And so this tradition can continue throughout the years, without threat from outside forces or the whims of fate and fortune, I have also enclosed—

"Do you know what these are?" Mrs. Hutchins gasped as she finished scanning the bundle of papers from the envelope. "Do you have any idea? This is it, Marty."

"What?"

"This is a list of every artist and architect who contributed to the school's renovation. Documentation, notarized. And believe me, it's quite a list. Unbelievable."

"Can I read this? I'm kind of at that part," Laurie said.

"Let the girl read," Mr. Wallace said. Laurie shot him a grateful look and went on.

> *I have also enclosed a list for your records. My fine and devoted friends generously poured their hearts and souls into the development of this school. Their skill and creativity are unrivaled and will serve as inspiration for our students for years to come. And as for Hilda, she may not be beautiful, but our guardian has served us well. But as my skills are not of an artistic nature, my dear friend Pablo has provided an alternative sketch, should you choose to display that instead.*
>
> *You have inspired me with your hard work. I hope Tuckernuck Hall will serve as inspiration for you in the years to come.*
> *Your devoted founder,*
> *Maria Tutweiler*

Laurie looked up at Mrs. Hutchins. "Pablo?"

Mrs. Hutchins held up the list. "Picasso. She really did know him."

"Surely we would've noticed a work by Picasso in the school." Principal Winkle frowned.

Mrs. Hutchins pointed to the first name. "He's on the list."

Principal Winkle peered into the frame and carefully pulled back the cardboard backing. Nestled in between the cardboard and the painting was a bold sketch of a chicken that could've been Hilda in better days.

"It's signed and everything. It's just like his dove sketches," Mrs. Hutchins whispered reverently. "Except it's . . ."

"It's a chicken," Bud said. He shook his head at Laurie. "I don't think we're going to be able to get rid of the Clucker mascot, Laurie."

Laurie shrugged. "I think you're right," she said, grinning. Being a Clucker didn't seem so bad anymore. Actually, it hadn't seemed that bad since they'd started on the whole treasure hunt.

"Henry Moore, James Earle Fraser, Charles Eames." Mrs. Hutchins stared back down at the list. "The names on this thing. Unbelievable. She listed everyone who contributed to the renovation, no matter how big or small their role." She chuckled. "Look—Fraser made the bust of Homer!"

Laurie snuck a peek at the list. Mrs. Hutchins was kind of hogging it. "Who's that guy? Millard Smoot?"

"According to this, he carved the presidents in the history wing." Mrs. Hutchins smiled. "Not everyone who helped with the renovation turned into someone famous. Maria Tutweiler had a lot of friends in the artistic and architectural communities." She narrowed her eyes at Principal Winkle. "They can't tear this place down."

"Oh, trust me, they won't," Principal Winkle said, picking up the phone again. "*Daily Herald*, please?" He held his hand in front of the receiver. "Walker LeFranco won't know what hit him."

Note from Walker LeFranco to Calliope Judkin

Calliope —
What part of "be my eyes and ears
at the school" didn't you understand?
You WASTED my time on gerbils and
petty squabbles while the STORY OF
A CENTURY passed you by. You can
forget about any introductions to
my contacts at the Morning News. We
could have prevented this, Calliope.

I don't know what I expected from a Judkin. You were never Hornet material.

No longer a Secret School Source,
Walker LeFranco

Note from Calliope Judkin to Walker LeFranco

Just because you're my neighbor doesn't mean you can push me around. I don't need your stupid contacts to be a reporter. Besides, Cluckers are cooler than Hornets any day.
Calliope
P.S. You can mow your own lawn from now on.

Note tossed by Calliope Judkin to Bud Wallace

So is it true that you guys are in charge of the school now? That's what they were saying in second period.

Note tossed by Calliope Judkin to Bud Wallace

Is it true that they're selling the Picasso to save the school? And do you and Laurie really get a cut of the profits?

Note tossed by Calliope Judkin to Bud Wallace

Are you really going to change the mascot to the Tuckernuck Flame-Throwing Iguana Spawn? 'Cause that's what they're saying in gym.

Note from Bud Wallace to Calliope Judkin

I'm sorry, Calliope, but I only like you as a friend. I'm sorry if that breaks your heart.
Bud

Note thrown by Calliope Judkin at Bud Wallace

I'm a REPORTER and INVESTIGATOR, you nitwit. I was UNDERCOVER. You think I've been following you guys because I LIKE YOU?

I got a tip from a source about a story,
that's it!
(Is it true that you and Laurie were given
baby chicks descended from the original
Hilda?)

Note from Marshall Deal to Bud Wallace

Mr. Wallace,
We've discussed your note passing before.
Things have not changed simply because you
have discovered the Tuckernuck Treasure.
Perhaps you'd care to discuss your note
passing with Principal Winkle?
Yours,
Marshall Deal
Sixth-grade science

Note from Principal Winkle to Bud Wallace

MR. WALLACE:
I UNDERSTAND YOUR INTEREST IN WHO
WILL BE SPEAKING AT THE EIGHTH-GRADE
GRADUATION CEREMONY, BUT WE WON'T

BE MAKING THAT DECISION FOR A WHILE
YET. MOST LIKELY IT WON'T BE UNTIL YOUR
CLASS REACHES THE EIGHTH GRADE. I'LL
DEFINITELY KEEP YOU IN MIND AND INFORMED.
  THANKS.
  YOUR PRINCI"PAL,"
  MARTIN WINKLE

Letter from Calliope Judkin to Olivia Hutchins

Dear Mrs. Hutchins:
I hereby resign my position as Gerbil Monitor
Number Three. I am no longer planning to get
a gerbil as a pet and would prefer to resume
my original duties of Office Liaison instead.
  Thank you,
  Calliope Judkin
P.S. You may want to seek therapy for
Ponch and Jon. Those gerbils are seriously
disturbed.

Note from Misti Pinkerton to Laurie Madison

Scavenger hunt? School project? A "thing"? The way I see it, I solved at least one of those clues for you, so I figure I've earned a place on the planning committee for next year's hunt. Believe me, I've got some awesome ideas for clues.

  Cluck cluck!

  Misti

EMAIL

FROM: LAURIE MADISON

TO: KIMMY BARANSKI

RE: Are you EVER transferring??

Hey Kimmy,

Nope, I think I'm just going to stay here and be a Clucker. You know, since I found the treasure and all.

See you,

Laurie

P. S. Want me to teach you the Clucker song?

Letter from Calliope Judkin to the editor-in-chief of the Daily
Herald

Dear Sir,
I am offering you the story of a lifetime: the
inside scoop on the hunt for the Tuckernuck
Treasure, as observed from day one by this
intrepid reporter.
Think about it. This is a limited-time offer.
    Calliope Judkin

Note from Laurie Madison, stuck to Jack Madison's door

I seem to remember a little bet about
whether I'd find the treasure. Something
about laundry?
    Time to pay up.
    Laurie

Note from Jack Madison, stuck to Laurie Madison's door

So, do you bleach your whites or not?
Just checking.
    Jack

EMAIL

TO: FLORA DOWNEY, Tuckernuck Hall

FROM: HORACE WALLACE SR.

SUBJECT: My Heartfelt Appreciation

Dear Miss Downey,

I want to thank you again for taking Bud under your wing and helping with his mathematics education. He is a changed boy. Would you allow me to take you to dinner on Friday to show my appreciation?

Yours,

Horace Wallace

EMAIL

FROM: FLORA DOWNEY, Tuckernuck Hall

TO: HORACE WALLACE SR.

SUBJECT: It's a Date

Wally,

I'd love to. And call me Flora.

Best,

Flora

Note from Horace Wallace Sr. to Horace Wallace Jr.

Hi, Bud,

I found a bunch of board games in the attic
that we boxed up awhile ago. Why don't you
invite a couple of your friends over to see if
they all still work?

Have a good day at school.

Your dad

P.S. Your old dinosaur toys were in there too.
I left them on your desk. T. rex says hi.

Note from Misti Pinkerton to Bud Wallace

If one of those board games is Risk, you and
Laurie are GOING DOWN.

Just a warning.

Misti :-)

Open Letter to School District

With this letter, I hereby tender my resignation as the president of the school board. In light of recent events, I feel my services would be put to better use elsewhere.

Walker LeFranco

Post-it on Principal Winkle's computer

Bad news, Marty. Some of the kids got a tip and stormed the staff room. They found the doughnuts. They know, Marty. They know.

Betty

Sign on cafeteria door

Due to recent allegations of unfairness re:
sweets, Tuckernuck Hall will now allow the
consumption of one (1) standard-sized dessert
per student at lunchtime. I hope that this
compromise will be satisfactory to all students.
Thanks.
Your Princi"PAL,"
Martin Winkle

Thank-you note left on Martin Winkle's desk

Marty,
Ponch and Jon just LOVE their Deluxe
Gerbil Playhouse! They are changed gerbils. I
have never seen them so calm and relaxed—
they spend their days playing on the wheel,
running through their access tubes, jingling
the bells, and swinging on the swing. You've
got to come by and see them!
Their door is always open.
Thanks,
Olivia

Note to Olivia Hutchins from Principal Winkle:

PLEASE TELL ME YOU'RE KIDDING ABOUT
THEIR DOOR.
MARTY

Maria Tutweiler locked the doors to Tuckernuck Hall one last time and tugged them to make sure they were secure. She had hoped to see her challenge through to the end, but the difficulties with the school board had made that an impossibility. She smiled to herself as she went to hand over her keys to the second principal of Tuckernuck Hall. It didn't matter if she was there to see it. She had set the wheels in motion, and she knew her students wouldn't let her down. That puzzle was as good as solved.

ACKNOWLEDGMENTS

This book would not have been possible without some amazing people—Katherine Tegen, Katie Bignell, Steven Malk, and the team at Katherine Tegen Books. You guys rock.

More thanks are in order:

To Elizabeth Enright, John Bellairs, and Ellen Raskin, for their books full of clues and mysteries.

To Wilkie Collins, for the use of the name.

To Washington and Lee University, for the use of the fight song (cluckerized though it may be).

To the pet store clerk in Richmond, for not being able to tell boy gerbils from girl gerbils.

And to Chuckie and Nibbles and their enormous brood of bruisers.